WITHOUT REASON

JOANNE RYAN

Tamarillas Press

ISBN: 9798515634568

Cover Design: © Joanne Ryan

CHAPTER ONE

I t might not be much, but it's home.

These words pop into my head as I close the front door on the last of the removal men. When the last of the boxes were deposited in the kitchen, the one who seemed to do all of the bossing around but the least amount of work hung around and attempted to make conversation with me. He'd not spoken one word to me before that so I knew he was waiting for a tip. I duly obliged with a crisp, new, twenty pound note. I don't know if it was my imagination but he seemed to look at it with disappointment. I was about to give him another twenty but stopped myself just in time when I remembered; I don't do that anymore. To prove to myself that I wasn't being mean I mentally applied the *people pleaser test* and confirmed to myself that twenty pounds was more than enough; I'd already paid the removal company over six hundred pounds to move my scant possessions less than ten miles across town.

Not that he knew any of this, of course; he simply stuffed the note into his pocket and strode down the hallway and out of the front door. It was only when he'd gone that I realised he hadn't even said thank you. Which made me extra pleased that I hadn't given him anymore but also slightly pissed off that I'd given him a tip at all.

Determined not to waste any more time wondering about suitable tips I walk down the long, narrow hallway and into the kitchen at the back of the house. The numerous cardboard boxes have been dumped around the room and I try not to feel depressed at the prospect of unpacking them all; a job only slightly less depressing than filling them up in the first place.

I give myself a mental shake; I have a new home and a new life and it's mine to do with as I wish. If I wanted to I could leave all of the unpacking and simply live out of boxes and wear pyjamas for the rest of my life. I won't, but I could if I wanted to.

Mine.

Not ours, I remind myself, not his, but *mine.*

And it's paid for; I could have had something nicer, grander and in a better area but for that I'd have needed a mortgage which would have tied me to something else that I no longer want – my old job. I can live comfortably on the remainder of my savings whilst I try and make a go of my own business.

This house may not be grand or posh but it's a sturdy, well built house. Built in the nineteen-thirties when things were made to last, it managed to remain standing despite world war two so that's good enough for me. It also has the added benefit of a good sized garden, both front and back. The kitchen and bathroom aren't new but they're of high quality and have been well looked after so there's really nothing that needs replacing.

I take a deep breath and grab hold of the box nearest to me and run my front door key down the tape to split it open. It's full to the brim with crockery and I take out the bright yellow plates and dishes and unwrap each one before carefully placing them on the work top. Once the box is empty I flatten it down and lean it against the wall by the back door but then change my mind. I may as well start as I mean to go on otherwise the kitchen will be filled with cardboard. I open the back door and the bright May sunshine greets me as I step outside. I stand for a moment and enjoy the sun on my face before grabbing the flattened-down box and dragging it over to the dustbin and laying it on the ground. The garden isn't very wide but it is long. The patio of mottled paving slabs that I'm standing on is uneven and I can feel one of them rocking underneath my feet. They'll do; I have no grand plans for the garden although I will have to get myself a lawnmower or the large lawn will soon get out of control.

At the very end of the garden is a prefab garage whose doors open out onto the narrow alley that runs along the back of the houses. I definitely have plans for this as it's going to be my workshop and is one of the reasons that I bought the house.

I head towards the garage and glance over into my neighbour's garden as I walk. Their garden is glorious; immaculate flower beds abound with colour and there are numerous pots full of healthy looking shrubs. The lawn is a mirror image of my own but unlike my spiky grass theirs would put a bowling green to shame. The waist high ancient breeze block wall between our gardens affords me and my neighbour no privacy at all but I'm not bothered; provided my neighbour doesn't accost me every time I step out into my garden, I can live with that. The neighbour on the other side of me is a different story; a high wooden fence runs the length of the garden and it must be at least seven feet high so they obviously like their privacy. The fence looks newly erected and I'm pleased that I won't have to creosote it or treat it anytime soon. I'm assuming that as my next door neighbour owns the fence they would have to do that, although I really have no idea as I used to leave all of that sort of stuff to Tom. I make a mental note to Google it.

I reach the garage and peer through the side window; I can't get in there as the key to the garage side door is in the house. Thankfully the garage seems completely empty and even the window appears to have been cleaned. I had a sneaking suspicion that the previous owner might leave her rubbish in there but it appears pristine.

I'm time-wasting.

I about turn smartly and march briskly up the path and back to the house; time to get on with things. Getting on with things is on my life plan list of things to do. A life plan might sound very grand but it's a very short list; do what I want, do a job I love, make new friends and get on with life. It's not even an actual list and exists only in my head. There is only one *don't* on there – no more people pleasing; I'm no longer going to be doing stuff that I don't want to do just to keep other people happy.

Once I'm back in the kitchen I open up another box and continue my unpacking onto the worktop until I run out of space. I need to get this put away before I can unpack anything else. The plates are new as is most of the kitchen equipment; I left far better quality behind but I wanted new, none of the old stuff that brings it's memories along with it. I know that Tom would have hated the bright yellow crockery so maybe that's why I bought it. There's no dishwasher here either so I'll be re-acquainting myself with the kitchen sink after many years absence.

For all that the house is modest and small, it's been very well cared for and I've no need to decorate as the walls are all painted a neutral colour and the carpets are spotless. I like old stuff; just because it's old it doesn't mean that it's no good anymore and I'm making a living out of old stuff so it's only right that I'm living in an older house.

I'm no longer going to be a sensible accountant but am jumping feet first into up-cycling and selling furniture.

I was very lucky to get this house at an absolute bargain price; the owner was keen to sell quickly as she was moving to start a new life in Australia – not that she told me that herself – that information was supplied by the garrulous estate agent who showed me around on my first viewing. For all his probing questions I made sure to tell him absolutely nothing of my own situation as I had no wish for my circumstances to be broadcast (and no doubt embellished) to the owner of every house that I viewed.

I'll admit that I was shocked when my first offer was accepted, it was low to the point of being insulting and I fully expected to have to pay more and intended it only as an opening offer. The fact that she accepted it immediately did give me pause for thought and I wondered if there was something about this house that the estate agent wasn't telling me. I made sure to pay for a full survey as I didn't want any nasty surprises but the house came back with a clean bill of health. I told myself that I needed to stop being so suspicious and be grateful that I would have extra money in my savings account.

I did eventually meet the owner when I made an appointment for a second viewing and she was reserved to say the least. I tried to engage her in conversation about Australia but she gave monosyllabic answers and I gave up in the end. I couldn't imagine someone so timid being brave enough to move to the other side of the world and start afresh. It occurred to me later that perhaps I shouldn't have let her know that I knew she was moving abroad; perhaps it was a secret that the big-mouthed estate agent was supposed to keep.

I fill the sink with hot soapy water and dunk the crockery in, once I've rummaged through another box and found some tea towels I dry it all and stow it away neatly in the cupboards. The cupboards are immaculate and I'm grateful that I don't have to start cleaning before I fill them up. The hours fly by as I slip into the routine of unpacking and finding homes for everything. Once the kitchen is straight I move into the lounge and begin on the boxes in there. It's only when my stomach starts to rumble that I realise that it's nearly seven o'clock and I haven't eaten anything since I had breakfast at the crack of dawn this morning.

I flop down onto the sofa and survey the room with satisfaction. The lounge is small and with my two sofas and large sideboard there's little room for anything else – but what else do I need? The television is sitting on top of the sideboard and the recessed bookshelves that sit on either side of the log burner will be more than big enough to hold my books and ornaments when I've finished unpacking them. There are only two more boxes in here left to do but they can wait until tomorrow. The small dining room between the lounge and kitchen will be staying empty for a while as I have no furniture to go in there. One of my first up-cycling jobs will be for myself – a table and chairs.

The evening sunlight is streaming through the window and I feel a sprig of optimism; maybe being on my own won't be so bad, maybe this new life can be a good life. The house is cosy and has a good feel about it; so perhaps, with time, I *can* be happy again.

I haul myself off the sofa and go out to the kitchen and root through the food cupboard for something to eat. I didn't bring very much in the way of provisions as I intend to do a big shop once I'm settled so there isn't much to choose from. I have bread, milk and tins of soup but my hands bypass the sensible options and settle on a packet of doughnuts. They'll do; I simply cannot be bothered to make dinner even if it would only require heating a tin of soup.

Do I really want them? I ask myself.

You bet I do.

Tom would be disgusted with me if he could see me now - not that we even had such food as doughnuts in the house but luckily, I no longer have to consider what he thinks. I push the thought of him away and tell myself that I'm not going to keep thinking about him; he is in the past and I need to focus firmly on the future.

I go back into the lounge and sit on the sofa and put my feet up. I eat three doughnuts straight from the packet and they're delicious; maybe I'll have the other one for breakfast. I'm not a binger and I'm not overweight but sometimes a doughnut or two is infinitely more attractive than cooking a meal for one. Tomorrow I'll go shopping and get some proper food.

But it won't be for kale smoothies, Tofu, or any of that muck.

From now on I'm doing, and eating, exactly what *I* want.

CHAPTER TWO

I've got a job.

I know, I know, I was going to work for myself and no one else but life happens, and it came about by complete accident so was obviously meant to be.

It all started this morning when I decided that I would start my new life by going for a walk and having a proper look around the neighbourhood. Apart from going out to do a big supermarket shop on Saturday I hadn't left the house all weekend as I'd been so busy getting everything straight.

The sun was shining, the air was warm and pleasant so I headed off down the street in the direction of the line of shops that I remembered driving past on my way here. There was also the possibility that I might bump into some of my new neighbours so it would be an opportunity to introduce myself to them. As it turned out I didn't see anyone at all which was a bit disappointing but it was a pleasant fifteen-minute stroll which had other unexpected results.

A newsagents, bookies, chip shop and a mini market were aligned in a row looking out over a stretch of scrubby grass. The shops looked neat, tidy and well cared for although there was one unit that was empty; it was previously a greengrocers but it now had a *for rent* sign plastered across the newspaper covered windows.

I made a note of the chip shop opening hours for the future (closed on Mondays) and then went into the mini market to get some milk. For a small shop it was very well stocked with pretty much any-thing that a person could need. I felt a bit bad that I was only buying milk but there was absolutely nothing else I needed as I'd practically bought the whole of Tesco's on Saturday. I resolved to try and do at least some of my shopping there in the future to support a local business.

I picked up the milk and went to the only till in the shop to pay. I couldn't help noticing the large, hand-written sign taped to the front of the till ad-vertising a job vacancy. As I handed over a five pound note for my milk I asked the cashier about it in an attempt to make conversation (another new resolution on my list; be more outgoing and try harder to make new friends) and the woman's face lit up.

'Are you interested?' Phoebe – the name on her badge – asked.

I opened my mouth to say no and then closed it again to have a think about it. I may add *thinking about stuff properly* to the list of things about myself that I need to change (instead of jumping in feet first and asking questions later or doing something and regretting it for the rest of my life).

'It's only for four mornings a week, Monday to Thursday,' she continued when I didn't answer. 'Eight until twelve, nine pounds an hour.'

That would be a hundred and forty-four pounds a week, my accountant's brain mentally calculated. Not to be sniffed at for basically standing around behind a till for four hours. It would be a commitment to get me out of bed in the mornings and add some structure to my day. Having had a regular nine to five job for so many years I live in terror that I'll resort to loafing around all day and lose the momentum to start anything. I'd still have the rest of the day and three full days on Friday, Saturday and Sunday to make a start on my up-cycling business. The walk here every day would be a bit of exercise, too, as it's hardly worth driving here.

'I've never worked in a shop before.' I eventually answered, expecting her to be immediately disinterested in me.

'But you are interested?' Phoebe asked in what I realised was a rather desperate manner.

'Well,...'

'Full, on the job training provided,' she added.

It would also mean that I wouldn't have to dip into my savings; over six hundred pounds a month would more than cover my household bills.

'How do I apply?' I asked.

'Just fill this in,' Phoebe answered as she produced a sheet of paper with a flourish from under the counter. 'I've got a pen if you want to do it now.' She pulled a biro from her pocket and offered it to me.

So I stood there and filled in the scant details required; basically my name, date of birth and address, my last period of employment and two references. I stumbled for a moment on the references; not because I don't have anyone to put but because I didn't know if I wanted my ex-boss to know that I'd applied for a job in a mini market. I then reminded myself that in my new life I wasn't supposed to be caring what other people think of me anymore so I wrote his name in the box and left the space for another reference, blank.

'I've only put one reference,' I said as I handed the form back to her. 'I worked for the same company for the last eighteen years so anywhere I worked before that wouldn't remember me. I can give you a personal reference if that's not sufficient.'

Phoebe took the form from me and read it slowly.

'You're an accountant?' she asked, in surprise.

'Yes,' I replied.

I could see the faintest glimpse of suspicion in her eyes – why would someone leave a well-paid job as an accountant to work in a mini market?

'I was made redundant,' I lied, although I'm not

quite sure why.

'I see,' she said, not seeing at all.

By now I was starting to regret the whole thing as it was becoming embarrassing and I was rapidly going off the idea. I was wondering how I could tell her in a nice way that I'd changed my mind when Phoebe suddenly slapped the form down onto the counter and stared at me intently.

'Would you like the job?' she asked.

'Um, yes, I think so,' I said, without quite meaning to.

'Great!' she said with a smile. 'And could you start straight away?'

'Yes,' I said.

'Excellent! The job's yours. How does tomorrow morning at eight o'clock, sound?'

'Um, good?'

'Excellent!' she repeated again. 'And make sure you bring your passport with you.'

'Passport?' I stared at her, I never imagined that international travel would be in the job description of a part-time shop assistant's role.

''Yes, for proof of ID.'

'Of course,' I said, feeling like a complete fool and proving that it's a very long time indeed since I've applied for a job. 'But don't you want to check my reference and interview me properly?'

'*That* was the interview,' she said, waving her hand dismissively in the air. 'And as for references, I'm a good judge of character so that's all the reference that I need.'

'Oh. Okay. I'll see you tomorrow then,' I said as she handed me my change.

'Perfect!' she said.

And that, as they say, was that.

* * *

On the way home I turn the corner into my street and I can see that there's someone in the front garden of the house next to mine. As I get closer I see that it's an elderly man and he's on his knees carefully clipping the edges of his immaculate lawn with a pair of garden shears. An elderly white terrier is laid on the grass asleep next to him. I slow my walk to a crawl and stop in front of the brick wall surrounding his garden.

'Hello there,' I say, leaning on the wall.

'Oh, hello,' he says, looking up at me with a smile. He slowly clambers to his feet, dusting his hands off as he does so. The terrier raises its head and studies me for a moment and then puts its head back on its paws and closes its eyes.

'Pleased to meet you.' He holds out his hand. 'I'm Bert.'

'Nice to meet you, Bert. I'm Frida, I've just moved in next door to you.'

We shake hands solemnly.

'I saw the removal van here on Friday so I guessed you were in. That's an unusual name these days,' he says. 'Frida.'

I smile. My name is actually Anni-Frid, but

everyone calls me Frida. My mother, in her typical getting it wrong fashion, intended to name me after the blond singer in Abba but got the wrong singer and named me after the dark haired one instead. I'm thankful for her mistake because as much as I hate Anni-Frid, it's at least better than Agnetha. I tell Bert none of these boring details.

'I blame my mother,' I say, with a smile.

'The old names are the best. So, Frida, how are you settling in?'

'Very well, thank you. I'm pretty much straight now even though I only moved in on Friday. I'm just getting my bearings in the neighbourhood and getting the lie of the land.'

'Oh, this is a good area,' he says. 'Me and my Doris, God rest her soul, moved in here as newlyweds nearly sixty years ago. There's not much goes on around here that I don't know about.' He looks wistful and rather sad at the same time. I'm guessing by his remark that Doris is no longer with us.

'That's good to hear. You have a beautiful garden there, Bert. I can see that I'll have to pull my socks up and sort mine out so I don't bring the area down.'

Bert beams and looks around proudly at his bowling green lawn and immaculate rose borders.

'Well, it keeps me busy you know, gives me something to do.'

'And,' I say, glancing over at the neighbour on the other side of my house. 'I can see that my other neighbour also has green fingers. You both put me to shame.'

Bert is about to answer me when a loud voice from behind makes me jump.

'Nothing to do with me,' the loud voice almost shouts. 'That's Bert's handiwork, too.'

I turn around and a tall, rather large woman is towering over me and invading my personal space and frankly, getting far too close for my liking.

'Oh, hello,' I say, shuffling backwards along the wall slightly to try and put some space between us.

'Diana,' she says, thrusting a meaty hand towards me. 'Your next door neighbour on the *better* side.'

'Frida,' I say, as I take her hand.

She bursts into loud laughter and briskly pumps my hand up and down before suddenly dropping it.

'Frida? Good God who inflicted that on you?' Before I can answer she continues. 'Bert here does my garden for me, DON'T YOU BERT.' She turns her head and shouts at Bert as if he's a half-wit before turning back to me. 'So. Are you all sorted?'

For a moment I wonder what she's talking about and then I realise what she means.

'Pretty much. Still a few things to do but I'm getting there.'

'And where do you work?' she demands.

'I'm self-employed.'

'Self-employed?' she echoes, as if I've just told her I'm an axe-murderer. 'So *what*, exactly, do you do?'

I open my mouth to answer her but then close it again, firmly. There's something about her that makes me feel as if I'm being interrogated and that I have to tell her but it's actually none of her business.

She stares at me and I'm sure her eyes narrow.

'Oh, this and that,' I eventually reply, annoyed that I caved in and answered her at all.

'This and that,' she repeats slowly as she continues to stare. 'Well, we'll have to talk about that. We'll get together for a coffee sometime this week and get to know each other properly. I'll let you know when I'm free.'

I stifle a laugh and nod politely, having absolutely no intention of having a get together with her. I don't know her but I instinctively know that she's not my sort of person and I don't want to meet up with her. I'm going to start as I mean to go on and nip this in the bud before it gets out of hand and I'm frightened to step outside of the house for fear of being talked into doing stuff I don't want to do. The old me would have felt obliged to have coffee with her every time she asked whilst hating every single minute of it. Forgetting the *thinking about stuff properly* rule, I've already decided that she's not the sort of person I want to be friends with; she's far too bossy and forceful. I have the distinct feeling that if I show a willingness to be friends I'll never get her out of my house and she'll be around every day bossing me about. Maybe I'm being unfair but there it is; she's only my neighbour – I don't *have* to be friends with her. Bert, on the other hand, can come in for a cup of tea any time he likes. I sneak a sideways look at Bert and he briefly meets my eye before hastily looking away.

'So. I must get on,' Diana announces loudly. 'Things to do. I have a proper job with proper hours so I can't afford to hang around gossiping all day. I'm only home now because I've taken the afternoon off. I'll let you know about that coffee.' And with that she clomps past me and continues to her front garden and lets herself in through the gate. I wait until she's unlocked her front door and is inside her house before turning back to Bert.

'Well, Bert, it was lovely meeting you.'

'You too, Frida.'

Bert picks up his garden shears and resumes his clipping and I continue up the path to my garden. As I'm putting my key in the front door lock a movement catches the corner of my eye and I have the definite feeling that someone has hurriedly moved away from next door's front window.

Diana.

Thank God there's a seven foot high fence between us.

CHAPTER THREE

I've only just got in from my second day at the mini market when the front door bell shrills. I kick my canvas shoes off in the kitchen and pad down the hallway in my bare feet. The job is hardly taxing but I'd forgotten what it's like to be on my feet for hours at a time; maybe I'll wear trainers tomorrow.

'I wondered how long you'd be able to stay away,' I say, as I pull open the front door.

'That's a nice way to greet your mother,' Mum says, as she squeezes past me into the hallway in a cloud of perfume and hair spray.

I shut the front door and follow her down the hallway and into the kitchen.

'I haven't even been in here a week yet,' I say, as I pick the kettle up and fill it from the tap.

'You've been here six days and I realised that if I waited for an invitation I'd be waiting forever so I invited myself.'

'You don't need an invitation, you're my mum.'

'Well sometimes it's nice to be asked, you know. Anyway.' She rummages around in her expensive leather handbag. 'I've bought you a house warming present.'

I watch as she roots around and wonder what she can possibly have bought for a house that will fit into her handbag.

'Aha! Here it is!' She holds out a glossy square of paper to me with a flourish.

I take it and read it.

''A voucher for a manicure?' I say.

'Yes! Just what you need because I know you'll have neglected your nails with all of the packing and everything. It's the works – hot wax massage, full polish – or shellac, if you'd rather. There's even an option for falsies if your own nails are completely shot. Look, I've had mine done.' She holds her fingers out and wiggles her lavender coated nails at me. 'Don't they look fab?'

Infuriating as she is, I can't help laughing. Only my mum would think of giving a manicure as a house warming present.

'What's so funny?' she asks. Her perfectly shaped micro-bladed eyebrows would be pulled into a puzzled frown if the Botox allowed.

'Nothing,' I say. 'Thank you.' Luckily, she'll have forgotten all about it by next week as there's absolutely no point in having a manicure if I'm going to start stripping and painting furniture for my new business. Although I'll feel guilty if I don't use the voucher because it *would* be a complete waste of her money. Maybe I'll have the manicure before I start the furniture; there's no rush to start immediately now that I have my job in the mini market. I can send Mum a picture of my nails when they're done and then I won't have to feel bad.

She slips her jacket off and looks around for somewhere to put it.

'Haven't you got any furniture?' she asks.

'Not in here, no, there's no room for a table or anything. I've got a dining room through there although there's no furniture in there yet, either. You can hang it in the hallway, there are plenty of coat hooks out there.'

Mum pulls a face and carefully folds her jacket and drapes it over her arm. There's no way she'll hang her expensive jacket from a hook.

I pull two mugs out of the cupboard.

'Tea?' I ask.

'Please. Black. I'm watching my weight.' She says this as if it's something new; she's been taking her tea black and watching her weight for as long as I can remember. She gazes around the kitchen before walking into the dining room.

'It's not as bad as I thought it would be,' she calls as she walks through to the lounge.

Coming from Mum, that's a massive compliment. The kettle comes to the boil and I pour the water into the mugs, put milk in mine and carry them through to the lounge and put them on the tiny coffee table and sit down next to Mum.

'It's not in bad condition for an old house although I still don't understand why you didn't want a nice modern apartment like mine. I could have helped you with it – I have the money and it'll be yours and Benny's when I'm gone. I've never seen the attraction in all this old stuff myself.'

I don't say anything; this is an old argument and one that I'm not going to win. Mum lives in a new, swish apartment with every mod con available and cannot understand why I don't want the same. She also doesn't understand why I would want to up-cycle 'old tat' as she puts it, when I could have something lovely and brand spanking new. She says that I would think differently if I'd been brought up wearing her sister's cast offs and having to make do and mend, like she did. She doesn't refer to the fact that I used to live in a nice, new, executive house just as swish as hers.

'Talking of your brother,' Mum says, even though we weren't. 'Have you heard from him recently?'

'No,' I lie. I had a text from him last week but I don't tell Mum this as she'll be hurt that he hasn't texted her.

'No funny feelings about him?' she asks.

'No, but I'm sure he's fine. He's only in London, Mum, not the end of the earth.' Mum is convinced that because we're twins, Ben and I have some sort of telepathic connection and that if there's anything wrong with him, I'll know. We don't, although sometimes I wish that we did.

'If he just called me now and again I wouldn't

mind, I just need to know that he's okay.' Mum sniffs and looks hurt and I wonder if I should tell her he sent me the briefest text possible which consisted of *happy moving day sis*. I'm about to open my mouth but stop myself; Mum has caught me out like this before and I know that the resulting guilt trip will last for weeks as somehow it will be my fault that Ben didn't call her.

'You could text him?' I suggest. 'He does always reply to you.'

'Oh no, I'm not doing that, if my own son can't be bothered to contact me, I'm not going to beg.'

I pick up my tea and sip it.

As usual, even though Mum has come round to see me and my new house, somehow we're talking about my brother again.

'I suppose he's back with *her* again,' Mum says.

'I don't know Mum, although I wouldn't be surprised. You know he can't keep away from her.'

Benny has been in an on and mostly off relationship with Monica, an aspiring singer who hooks up with my brother mostly when she's out of work and has no money. Or somewhere to stay; she lives in house shares and has a habit of getting thrown out for not paying the rent. Ben has a tiny one bedroomed flat in Camden which is now worth a small fortune as the area has 'come up'. Mum's always begging him to come home as he could buy a big house here with what he'd get for his flat and still have cash to spare. It's not as if he even needs to live in London for his job; he works as a roadie for touring bands so can pretty much live anywhere. Much as I'd like him to live closer I honestly can't see him ever coming back while Monica is still in the picture. He's waiting for her to agree to settle down but I don't think that will ever happen. For some reason my brother is besotted with her and cannot see that she's been using him for the last ten years.

'Anyway, never mind your brother,' Mum says, getting up from the sofa. 'I didn't come here to talk about him. You can give me the guided tour now because I'm not going to be able to drink that tea for at least a fortnight, it's hotter than the sun. You should have put some cold water in out of the tap.'

Yes, and then you would have said it *tasted funny*. I put my mug down on the coffee table and stand up.

Mum looks me up and down and unexpectedly grabs hold of me and pulls me into a hug.

'I am proud of you, darling, even though I don't always show it.'

I return her hug and we stand silently for a moment.

'Your dad would be very proud of you, buying a house all on your own and getting on with life after everything that's happened. He always said you had guts.'

I say nothing; I wouldn't say I had guts at all. The fact is that I didn't have any choice *but* to get on with things.

'Come on, then.' I slowly disentangle myself

from her arms. 'I'll show you around.'

I'm about to turn away when Mum stops me.

'Where is it?' she asks with something like panic in her voice. 'Where's your locket?'

I pat my neck and laugh.

'Don't panic, Mum, it's quite safe. It's in my jewellery box upstairs, I just haven't put it on yet.'

'Oh, that's a relief,' she says. 'I thought for a horrible moment there that you'd lost it.'

* * *

Several mugs of tea later, I close the front door on Mum and she zooms off in her brand new BMW. She's going into town to meet her friend Susie for some shopping and maybe an early dinner afterwards.

To give Mum her due, she was complimentary, – in her own way –about my house. She called the bathroom 'retro' but didn't slag it off and she did agree with me that the whole place had been left in an immaculate condition. She thought I could definitely *do something* with the garden and said that I should get some advice from Bert next door when I told her that I'd been chatting to him.

There was a bit of a sticky moment when I told her about my job in the mini market. I thought of not telling her because Mum would never set foot inside a mini market no matter how desperate she was; it's Waitrose or nothing for her. But I decided to tell her anyway because I knew that despite never being likely to see me there, somehow, she'd find out eventually. She has a way of finding out *everything* through her enormous network of friends and acquaintances and I'd rather that she heard the news from me than from someone else. As I expected, she couldn't understand why I would want to work in a *corner shop*, as she called it. Why, she wanted to know, had I given up a perfectly good, very well-paid job to go and work for minimum wage in a menial position? I said nothing, fronted it out and basically let her tell me how foolish and headstrong I've been and just nodded now and then. I knew that if I argued with her it would only prolong the agony and eventually she ran out of steam and muttered that I wouldn't last long when I realised how boring it was. How she knows this, I have no idea as she's never worked in a shop in her life.

But at least that conversation is out of the way now.

I stand for a moment in the hallway and run through what I need to do now. I started searching my bedroom last night and I need to continue that before I begin looking in the rest of the house. When I told Mum that my locket was in my jewellery box it was a lie; I can't find it anywhere. I only ever take it off at night when I go to bed and I always leave it on the windowsill in the bathroom and put it straight on after my shower in the morning. This has always been my routine and even though I've moved around I've stuck to the same routine and still continued with it when I moved here.

At least I thought I had; when I got out of the shower yesterday morning it wasn't on the windowsill where I usually put it. For some reason I must have put it down somewhere else but I simply can't remember where. Mum and Dad gave me that locket for my twenty-first and it was one of Dad's first purchases when he set up his antique jewellery business. To say that it has sentimental value would be an understatement; not only for me but for Mum as well. I console myself with the fact that it must be in the house somewhere and I just need to find it.

Because wherever it is, I *have* to find it.

CHAPTER FOUR

This is my third morning working in the mini market and I seem to be getting the hang of it. Phoebe is now confident enough to leave me on my own which allows her to carry on with her admin tasks in the back office. I call it an office but it's more like someone's lounge – It has an old, over-stuffed sofa and an ancient dining table with a computer on it which serves as a desk. I only go in there at the start and end of my shift to hang my coat and bag up as I'm the only one working in the shop in the mornings. When there aren't any customers in I'll come out from behind the till and straighten a few things on the shelves or put things back that people have picked up and then not bought. Most people would say that it's a dull job but I quite like it; the radio plays in the background and it feels as if I'm being for paid for doing very little. I was paid much more in my old job but I certainly earned it; when I compare what I'm doing now to the old stressful financial meetings and constantly changing deadlines, I know which I prefer. Phoebe brings a cup of coffee out to me at about ten o'clock and if there aren't any customers who want serving she'll stay and we'll have a chat until someone interrupts us by coming up to the till.

The job is hardly taxing; there are a spate of customers from eight until nine, which is mostly people on their way to work and parents dropping their children off at school. The rest of the morning is mostly mums with toddlers coming in for bits and pieces to supplement their big supermarket shops. From my short time here I can see that Phoebe must make a steady income from the shop and as well as me she has three other staff who help cover the weekend and evening shifts. Phoebe herself works most afternoons and has the weekends off – although she's never truly away from it as she lives in the flat above the shop. I assumed that she had a partner but she told me that she bought the shop on her own. She spent twenty years working her way around the big four supermarkets and has been a manager in all of them. I'm not much good at guessing people's ages but I think she's about forty-five, so a little bit older than me – or maybe I'm flattering myself.

I like working here; I've discovered that I'm more sociable than I thought and I seem to be able to chat to the customers without any trouble at all. Mostly people are friendly, apart from the odd misery first thing in the morning, but I can live with that.

Thankfully, I haven't seen Diana since Monday and I assume that she's at work so I haven't yet been summoned to have coffee with her. I've thought about her assumption that I'll go running when she calls and I've decided to employ Mum's fail-safe method of dealing with people that she doesn't want to socialise with; the cold shoulder. Basically, if Mum feels that someone is being over-familiar and encroaching on her personal space, she gives them the cold shoulder. This means that mum becomes ultra-polite and when unwanted in-vitations are issued she simply doesn't answer or continues to talk about something else as if she hasn't heard. She says that people soon get the message and it saves embarrassment all round. It might sound harsh, Mum says, but it's much kinder in the long run.

It does sound harsh and this is why I've never given anyone the cold shoulder in my life. I'm a softie who doesn't like to hurt other's feelings – usually to my own detriment.

Or as Mum would say; I'm a people pleaser.

She's right of course; thinking back over the years I can recall on many occasions being almost pinned against the wall whilst being verbally as-saulted by the person that everyone else avoids. If there's a crashing bore monopolising someone's time you can bet your life that the someone being bored to death will be me. I'm such a pushover that I'll even appear to be enjoying it; but that's going to change because I'm determined not to be a people pleaser any more. I've no wish to hurt Diana's feelings but equally, I have no desire to be lumbered with a friendship that I don't want. I know I've only met her briefly but I can tell from our short acquaintance that if I give her an inch, she'll take a mile and I'll be having coffee and doing things that I don't want to do all of the time. I'll end up frightened to step outside my house in case she's there and I can't have that.

Better to start as I mean to go on.

'So, what do you think of your first week?'

I look up from my position slumped over the counter to see that Phoebe has come out from her office and into the shop. I glance at my watch to see that it's nearly twelve o'clock.

'Good,' I say, with a smile. I realise that I mean it.

'Excellent!' Phoebe pops a brown envelope down on the counter. 'Your first pay packet although of course it's only for three days. From next week I'll pay it straight into your account but as you missed this week's run I thought you'd like the cash.'

'Thank you,' I say, picking up the envelope. 'I wasn't expecting to be paid until next week.'

'Oh, I don't expect you to wait a week. You've settled in so well, I hope you're going to come back next week.' She looks slightly worried when she says this.

'I definitely am coming back, it's great to do something totally different,' I say.

'Brilliant!' Phoebe says. 'I must say that you've

fitted in really well, it seems as if you've always been here!'

'Thank you.' It's nice of Phoebe to say this and actually, I do feel at home.

'It's just a shame I haven't come across your locket,' Phoebe says. 'Have you found it yet?'

'No, I haven't,' I say. 'I'm sure it's just a question of time. I don't think I lost it in here although thanks for looking. It must be in my house somewhere.'

'It'll turn up,' Phoebe says, confidently. 'You'll probably find it in the first place you looked – sometimes you just can't see for looking!'

'You could be right,' I laugh.

I hope she is.

* * *

'Piece of cake, Frida?' Bert asks as he puts two cups of tea on the small table in front of the sofa. Bert's dog, Barkley was snuggled up on the sofa next to me but as soon as Bert appeared from the kitchen he jumped nimbly down onto the floor.

'Oh, yes please. Just a small piece though, got to watch my weight.'

Bert goes back out to the kitchen and reappears minutes later with a tea plate with a large slice of Battenberg on it.

'There's nothing of you so you get that down you,' he says, as he hands the plate to me.

I take a bite and it's delicious; Battenberg is one

of my favourites from when I was a child; Ben and I used to fight over getting the piece with most of the marzipan on.

'This is lovely, Bert, where did you get it?'

'Get it? I didn't buy it, I made it. I was a master baker many moons ago. I knocked that up this morning.'

'Really? Well, it's amazing, the best one I've ever had,' I say.

Bert smiles and sits down in the armchair opposite me.

'I don't bake that often now – hardly seems worth it for one but when I knew you were popping in I thought I'd make the effort.'

'Well, I'm glad you did.' I pop the last piece into my mouth.

Bert invited me in for a cup of tea when I was out in the garden yesterday afternoon. He was digging his borders and we got chatting; he's so easy to talk to that I found myself telling him all about my new job and my plans for the future. I was actually going to ask him round to mine but he beat me to it. He's a lovely man and I'm pleased to have such a nice neighbour.

'So, Bert.' I swallow the last of the cake. 'Are you friendly with all of the street? Has anyone else been here as long as you?'

'Well,' he says, looking upwards as he thinks about it. 'Old Mrs Rogers at number two moved in about the same time as me and Doris. But she's gone into a home now and her son's been renting the place out and I can't say I know who lives there now. I'm on nodding terms with everyone but most of the street are at work all day so I don't really get to see them.'

It's true that most people seem to be away from the street during the day as there are hardly any cars in the street until six o'clock at night when the road starts to fill up. I've seen a few people about but most are content just to say 'hello' and continue on their way rather than stop for a chat.

'Not like it used to be,' he says, wistfully. 'Used to be a real community here at one time.'

'Times have changed,' I say. 'And not always for the better.'

'Very true,' Bert says, solemnly. 'But it's nice you've moved in – it's good to have some young blood about the place.'

'Young blood!' I laugh. 'I'm nearly forty!'

'That's young to me, so you make the most of it.'

We sip our tea in companionable silence and listen to the steady tick of Bert's wooden clock from the sideboard. There are lots of photographs in frames around the room and the sofa and armchair cushions are plumped just so. Bert looks after his home in the same way that he cares for his garden and it feels homely and cosy. It's not a bit like my brother's house where the fact that he's a man living on his own is evident in the lack of homely touches and inch thick dust everywhere. Even when Monica stays it's not any different, she lacks the homely touch too and simply dumps her piles of clothes onto the floor next to Ben's.

Bert's house reminds me of my late grandmother's house and I have a sudden longing to be a child again; the world felt so safe and secure then.

'Penny for them?' Bert asks.

'I was just thinking how lovely your home is.'

'Thank you. Doris always kept it just so and I don't want to let her down.'

There's silence for a moment.

'How long has she been gone, Bert?' I ask gently.

'Five years,' he says. 'And I still miss her every day.'

'Do the rest of your family live close by?' I ask. I've noticed that lots of the photographs around the room are of a blond haired girl ranging from toddler to adult.

Bert's face lights up and I'm glad I asked.

'Our Gena doesn't live near but we keep in touch by Facetime every week. She's in Australia,' he says, proudly.

'Wow, Australia,' I say. 'Has she been there long?'

'Eight years. I've got two grandchildren now as well, Brodie and Annette. Five and three they are and they're the spit of our Gena when she was a little 'un.'

'Have you not thought of going for a holiday, Bert?'

'Doris and I went the year after Gena and Phil moved there but I haven't been back since. Although Gena really wants me to go this summer – which is their winter – she says I should go for at least eight weeks to make it worthwhile.'

'You should definitely go!' I say.

'Oh, no, I couldn't. Bert shakes his head.

'Why not? You wouldn't have to ask me twice. It'd be the trip of a lifetime!'

Bert looks down at his cup. 'No. I couldn't.' He pauses for a moment. 'I couldn't leave the garden for that long.'

'Don't worry about that,' I laugh. 'I can look after it for you, although it won't be to your high standard. I could keep on top of it though until you come back.'

'It's...' Bert starts to say something but stops. 'I'm too old,' he states flatly.

I feel that I've said something wrong; the mood has changed and Bert seems despondent and lost in thought. I look down at Barkley lying on the floor and wonder if the real reason is his dog; Barkley's old and I don't supposed Bert would want to put him in kennels for two months in case he wasn't around when he came back. I decide it might be best to change the subject.

'So, Bert,' I say, after a few moments, trying to lighten the mood. 'Fill me in on the gossip, what was the previous owner of my house like as a neighbour? I only met her twice but she seemed a very private person, did you have much to do with her?'

Bert slowly stands up from the sofa and picks the empty cups and saucers up from the table.

'She was a very nice woman,' he says, quietly.

'Did you want another cup of tea or do you have to be going now?'

He doesn't say it in a rude way but he's asking me to go. I've said or done something wrong but I don't know what.

'Thank you, Bert, but I must be getting off. Lots to do, you know,' I say, brightly.

'Righto. I'll see you out.'

I follow him out of the lounge and into the hallway and he pulls the front door open.

'Take care,' he says, as I step outside.

'You too, Bert.' I turn and answer but he's already closing the door on me.

Whatever I said, it certainly hit a nerve.

He wouldn't even *look* at me.

CHAPTER FIVE

Diana catches me as I leave to go to the supermarket to get some steaks in for to-night's dinner. I've managed to avoid her all week but that's probably only because she's been at work. I've just locked the front door when I see her and my heart sinks but I take a deep breath and give her a big smile and remind myself; be like Mum.

I don't want to hurt Diana's feelings but equally, I'm determined not to be lumbered with her. On our very brief acquaintance it's obvious that she's not my sort of person – she's loud and overbearing and when faced with this I fear that I'll resort to my old mouse-like behaviour and let her trample all over me. I really don't want to go back to being like that.

Polite cold-shoulder, I repeat in my head as she strides purposefully towards me.

'Good morning!' she bellows as she gets closer.

'Morning,' I reply in my best cheerful manner.

'It's another lovely day.'

'It is,' she agrees. 'The best May that we've had for years.'

The sky is blue and the sun is already quite hot even though it's early. A good day to start my garden, I decide, and Ben can help too when he arrives. He's staying for the weekend and I'm sure he won't mind a bit of grass cutting.

Diana looks at her watch.

'I can fit you in around three for a coffee,' she says.

I open my mouth to speak but she continues talking.

'You can have a look at my tax return. It won't take you very long what with you being an accountant and everything so there'll be no need for you to charge me.'

I gawp at her; I can't help it, the bloody cheek of the woman. How does she even know that I'm an accountant?

'I'll see you at three o'clock sharp. Perhaps you could bring some cake with you? I'm not fussy but nothing with cheap icing on, thank you, I prefer real cream. Perhaps some biscuits too, the chocolate ones from the patisserie in the town are very nice; you could call in there while you're out.' With that she starts to walk away. I continue to gawp like a floundering fish before I finally manage to find my voice.

'I'm afraid I can't make it today. I'm busy.' In my determination to make sure she hears me the words come out much louder than I intended and I'm almost shouting at her.

She stops and slowly turns to face me and then walks back towards me. She keeps walking and I try not to feel intimidated as she again invades my personal space and gets much too close to me.

'Busy?' she repeats. She peers down at me and I curse the fact that I'm only five-foot two and have to look up at her as if I'm a small child and she's the grown up. Her peculiar pale grey eyes scrutinise my face and I force myself not to look away from her.

'Yes. I have my brother coming to stay for the weekend and we have an awful lot to do,' I say, in a jolly way, managing not to shout at her this time. I then fix a completely fake smile on my face. Before she can answer I step smartly backwards and turn on my heel.

'Perhaps we can do it another time,' I call out to her over my shoulder as I walk briskly towards my car. I can feel her eyes on me as I click the button to open the door and clamber into the car. I pull the door shut and quickly start the car up and zoom off down the road. I turn right at the end, going in the completely wrong direction in my haste to get away from her. As I pull out of the street I look in the rear view mirror and she's still standing there, watching me. I breathe a huge sigh of relief that I've made my escape; and I didn't even have to lie, either.

Which is good because somehow, I think she'd

have known I was lying.

I want to feel proud of myself for getting out of an unwanted invitation but I know that really I'm just fooling myself; I know that if Ben hadn't been coming I would have struggled to find a reason to refuse her invitation. I would more than likely have ended up going round for coffee *and* doing her tax-return for free and would probably have bought some expensive cakes and biscuits to take with me, too. I'm such a pushover.

I need a plan, apart from the cold shoulder; from now on I need to have an excuse ready whenever I leave the house at the weekend in case I bump into her or else I'm going to get caught out. If I make enough excuses she'll eventually get the message and tire of asking me.

Yes, that's all I need to do.

The polite cold shoulder and a convenient excuse – which is more than she deserves considering the cheek of her.

✳ ✳ ✳

I've bought plenty of steak for tonight's dinner as my brother can't have a meal without at least half of the plate being covered with dead animal. Not that I'm a vegetarian or anything but the amount that he eats for one meal would keep me going for at least a week.

I've also invited Mum for lunch tomorrow so that she can see her boy; when Ben arrives this afternoon I'll give him the usual lecture about contacting Mum more but I've no doubt it'll fall on deaf ears. He didn't mention Monica when he phoned and said he wanted to visit but I'm guessing that he and Monica are 'off' again. If Monica is on the scene he can never drag himself away from London to visit me or mum as he can't bear to be away from her. Monica never comes with him now; Mum and I have only ever been nice to her but I think she knows that we can see straight through her.

I unpack my shopping and wedge the steaks, beef and huge chicken that I've bought for tomorrow's lunch into the tiny fridge. I have a moment of anxiety as I remember that Mum is bound to notice tomorrow that I'm not wearing my locket; I still can't find it and I have an awful feeling that I'm not going to.

Shaking off the vision of Mum getting upset I unlock the back door and step outside into glorious sunshine and clear blue sky. I bought myself a new lawnmower and some sort of strimmer thing for doing the edges this morning. I have no idea what I was buying I just went for basic models that were cheap. I wish now that I'd picked up a couple of the sun beds that were on special offer in Tesco's; they would have been ideal for the garden. I don't even have any dining chairs that I can bring outside as the table and chairs that I've bought to go in the dining room have yet to be up-cycled. They're waiting patiently in the garage for me to make a start on them. I push down the rising panic that I should be doing them *now,* right this minute and stop time-wasting. This is something else to be added to my growing list of changes that I'm making to my life; there is no time limit on me or anything that I do. The old me would have fretted that there was furniture waiting to be done in much the same way that I could never leave house-work, a gym session or even a visit to a friend. My life was so organised that there was a schedule for everything and if I didn't see my friends on a regu-lar basis I feared that they would somehow forget me and un-friend me. The irony is not lost on me that now I never see them at all; they're still my friends but they're also Tom's and it all feels too awkward

Besides which, I'm pretty sure that they knew what Tom was up to long before I did.

All far too uncomfortable.

I amble over to the ancient wooden bench that the previous owner left – although it looks as old as the house so it was probably already here when she moved in. It sits underneath the kitchen win-dow and faces the garden. I plonk myself down and turn my face upwards to the sun.

Bert's back garden is empty and I haven't seen him out in his front garden either; I hope he's okay. He's usually pottering around in one or the other but I haven't seen him since I went in for a cup of tea on Thursday. I feel, somehow, that I've offended him but even though I've been over our chats a million times I can't think of anything that I've said that would have upset him.

As I sit and ponder, I decide that I'm going to go and knock on his door to make sure he's okay. He's getting on and I need to know that he's alright even if he doesn't want to chat to me. Decision made, I stand up to go and knock on his door when I hear the sound of his back door opening. Bert appears followed by Barkley trotting behind him.

'Bert!' I say, with a smile, walking over to the wall. 'How are you? I was just thinking about you.' I lean over and ruffle Barkley's head.

'I'm fine, and you?'

He seems as cheerful and as friendly as ever and I feel relieved; I may be giving my other neighbour the cold shoulder but I don't want to lose Bert's friendship. We may not have known each other for very long but I feel that we're friends already.

'I'm good, thanks,' I say, 'Just enjoying the lovely sunshine. I've got my brother coming for the weekend.'

'Ah, that's nice for you, it's nice to have your family around. He lives in London, doesn't he?'

'He does.' We continue to chat as if Thursday never happened. I'm tempted to ask him about him visiting his daughter but stop myself; I'm wary of inadvertently putting my foot in it again. I know that it must have been Bert who told Diana that I was an accountant as he's the only person who knows but I don't mention that either; I don't want it to sound as if I'm accusing him of something. It doesn't matter, he would have told her quite innocently, not realising that she'd expect free financial advice.

'I'll probably need some gardening advice from you when Ben arrives – I'm going to put him to work and get him to help me tidy up the garden.'

'Anything I can do, you just say the word. You've certainly picked the right weekend for it. It's going to be a hot one.' He gazes up at the sky and carefully rolls one shirt-sleeve up to his elbow before starting on the other.

'Oh, Bert,' I say. 'What happened?'

He pauses with his sleeve rolling and stares at me.

'Your arm? That looks really nasty.'

He looks down at his arm and at the large black bruise covering the area between his elbow and wrist.

'Oh, that?' he says, slowly. 'I fell over yesterday and knocked it.'

'Looks very painful,' I say, with concern.

He slowly rolls his sleeve back down over the bruise and buttons the cuff.

'Just a fall,' he says, without looking up. 'Nothing to worry about but I think I'll keep it covered because of the sun.'

'Why don't you come round and I'll make us both a cup of tea?' I suggest. He looks so frail and alone and I suddenly feel so sorry for him.

He continues to look down at his feet and doesn't answer.

'We could sit in the garden and drink it – I think I even have some chocolate digestives in the cupboard. We could have some before my brother arrives and eats them all. Or,' I say, when he doesn't answer. 'I could make us a sandwich instead, must be lunchtime by now.'

Bert looks up.

'That's a lovely offer, Frida, that really is, but I'm going to have to say no. I've got a bit of a headache to be honest so I think I'll go and have a bit of a lie down.' With that he turns and walks slowly back into the house, calls Barkley in and closes the door.

I stare after him. I definitely didn't say anything to offend him this time, did I? I carefully go over the brief conversation that we've just had and I can't think of anything that would cause offence.

And then it hits me.

I'm the one being over-friendly and he's giving *me* the cold shoulder.

CHAPTER SIX

No one would guess that Ben and I are brother and sister, let alone twins because we look absolutely nothing like each other. Ben takes after Dad and Mum says I take after her although I can't see it myself. We're not identical (that would be impossible) and when we were at school a lot of people thought we were cousins because we shared the same surname. We couldn't be more different, I'm five-foot-two with fair, curly hair and Ben is six-foot-two with dark brown, straight hair that refuses to stay flat and sticks up in tufts.

'Sis!' he shouts, beaming at me as I open the front door.

'Bro!' I shout, only not quite as loudly as I usher him in. No one is as loud as my brother. I feel a rush of happiness and realise that I've missed the big galumph.

'So,' he says, looking around as he stomps up the hallway. 'This is your new pad, then, eh? Not bad.'

He hurls his battered holdall in the direction of the stairs where it hits the wall and lands with a thud on the floor – he does all of this without pausing in his clomping through to the kitchen. He leans on the sink and gazes out of the window into the garden.

'Wow, love the garden, it's bloody massive. Wish I had a garden,' he says, wistfully.

'You could if you moved back here, you could probably buy a mansion from the sale of your flat,' I retort.

'That's a thought,' he says, quietly.

This is a surprise; normally when I say this he replies that he'd rather stick pins in his eyes than live here and die of boredom. I sense all is definitely not well in Monica-land as even when they've been apart he's never considered moving back home.

He turns and leans against the sink, facing me.

'How's it going? You settled in, everything okay?'

'I'm fine,' I say. 'I've even got myself a little job.'

'You don't do little jobs, you only do big jobs in big corporate companies,' he laughs. 'You're the sensible twin and I'm the wannabe-rock star who never grew up.'

'Nope,' I say, shaking my head. 'It's definitely a little job. I'm working some morning shifts on the till in a mini market and actually, I quite like it.'

'A mini market? Bloody hell, I was sure that after you jacked in at Bowden's you'd go and get yourself another important job somewhere else.' Ben folds his arms and stares at me. 'You are okay, though?'

'Yes, I'm fine. I've got a new life and I'm doing what I want for a change. I feel that I've turned a corner at last and I'm putting me first.'

'Good,' Ben says, unsmilingly. 'It's about time.'

It is indeed.

This time last year I was living my old married-for-ten-years-life with my husband Tom, blissfully unaware that from practically the day we got married he'd been cheating on me with his secretary. I would probably still be living that life right now if his secretary hadn't gone and got herself pregnant.

'Talking of pricks, have you heard anything from him?' Ben asks.

'Nope, why would I? Anyway, he doesn't know where I live and I've no intention of telling him.'

Ben always refers to Tom now as 'the prick'; he and Tom used to be the best of friends and I think Ben felt the betrayal almost as much as I did. I moved out of our new, huge, executive house on the day I discovered Tom's affair and I haven't seen him since. He did try; he came round to Mum's but I told her not to let him in or else I'd never forgive her so she sent him away with an earful. I insisted that all contact had to be by email or phone as I couldn't bear to talk to him as I was afraid that he'd manage to somehow make his behaviour *my* fault.

Yes, I was that pathetic; Tom knows me well and knew that I'd never forgive him – that's if he even wanted forgiveness. I know that he would try and justify himself because he thinks he can talk his way out of anything and I just didn't want to hear it. I felt bad enough without him confirming that I'd been such a crap wife that he'd had to have a bit on the side.

On reflection I think I actually made it easier for Tom as he didn't try *that* hard to persuade me to see him and I know that he didn't wait very long to shack up with the secretary because one of our friends let it slip. The secretary must be as pathetic as me to wait ten years for him. I wonder if she got pregnant deliberately to force him to make a commitment. It feels bizarre even now that one day I was living my normal, seemingly happily married life and the next I was camping out in Mum's spare room.

I wonder if he's still living in our marital home with her and their baby. I only went back to the house once and made sure that Tom was at work before I returned to pick up the few possessions – mostly clothes – that I wanted. I left that marriage with hardly anything because I couldn't bear to be reminded of ten years of deceit. Tom paid me my share of the equity of the house – which wasn't a lot considering how big our salaries were – but it was enough to buy this house outright. We should have had more than we did but gym memberships, top of the range cars, expensive meals out and luxury holidays abroad don't come cheap. Our huge mortgage never bothered us as we had the income to match and I, at least, thought that we had years ahead of us to pay it. If he's still living there he may be struggling now.

'What are you smiling about?' Ben asks.

'Nothing,' I say, unaware that I was.

I could look, of course, and see if he's still living in our old house with the secretary. It would be easy enough to find out but I've avoided all social media since we split up as I couldn't bear to see – even by accident – pictures of him with his new son or daughter. Although I still have Facebook on my phone and Tom is, weirdly, still one of my 'friends'. The divorce is done and dusted and one day I'll be totally over him, but that day hasn't come yet. I only hope that if I ever cross his path I see him first so I can avoid him.

'You can't avoid seeing him forever,' Ben says, reading my mind.

'Yes I can,' I snap. 'Just watch me.'

There's silence for a moment as Ben scrutinises my face.

'So. I'd better tell you,' he says, slowly.

'Tell me what?' I ask.

'The prick's been texting me. He wants your address.'

'What!' I shriek. 'You'd better not have told him, no way do I want him coming round here.'

'Of course I haven't told him. He says he needs to talk to you.'

'No he doesn't,' I say. 'We're divorced, remember? I have nothing to say to him and I'm not interested in anything he has to say.'

Ben shrugs. 'I'm just the messenger. It'd be a lot easier if you actually replied to his messages and then he'd stop blowing up *my* fucking phone.'

'I've blocked him,' I mutter. 'So his messages don't get through to me.'

'Then unblock him and deal with it and stop burying your head in the sand,' Ben says, grimly. 'Why are you so afraid of speaking or seeing him? You can't hide from him forever.'

Because I'm not sure I can cope, that's why. Maybe Ben's right and I need to face up to things so perhaps that's another thing to add to my list; stop hiding and being a coward.

'I'll think about it,' I mutter.

'So,' I ask after several minutes of silence, aware that I'm deflecting the conversation away from me. 'How's Monica?'

'Dead,' Ben says, without emotion.

I look at him in shock.

'To me,' he adds.

This is unusual; he *always* defends Monica. In all the years he's been with her he's never said a word against her or allowed Mum or me to slag her off; not that we would, we're not that stupid.

My brother is beyond loyal.

'What's happened?'

'She's been shagging another bloke.'

Mum and I have always known that Monica had other men; when she wasn't with Ben we knew she must be with someone else because she's incapable of being alone. But Ben had her on an impossibly high pedestal and would never believe badly of her.

'Are you sure?'

'Yep. Saw it with my own eyes,' he says. 'In my own bed.'

'Oh, God, how awful.'

'Yeah, wasn't much fun. She thought I was away for the weekend setting up a gig in Swansea but it got cancelled at the last minute.'

'So you're finished?' I ask.

'Yep. Didn't help that I wanted to smash the bloke's face in and she stopped me 'cos she didn't want him to get hurt. She practically dragged me off him.'

I imagine the scenario; my brother is a pretty threatening sight when roused to anger – it happens rarely but I wouldn't want to be in his way when it does.

'Ouch,' I say. 'So we've both been cheated on, now.'

'Yeah, great isn't it,' Ben says, grimly. 'It's not a club that I really wanted to join.'

'No chance of forgiving Monica?' I ask.

Ben shakes his head.

'None. Like I said, she's dead to me.'

He means it too; Ben and I may not look alike but we have the same outlook; he is no more capable of forgiving Monica for cheating than I am of forgiving Tom. I don't know if that's a good trait to have, but there it is.

'Maybe we should have a big bash for our fortieths,' Ben says. 'Show 'em we've still got what it takes and that *our* lives are beginning at forty.'

I think about this for a moment.

'That'll be great for you but crap for me – remember, all of my friends are now Tom and *her* friends so my list of people to invite will be you and Mum.'

'Invite them anyway, show them you don't give a shit.' Ben laughs.

'No thanks, I think I'll pass on that.'

'You don't need to invite anyone anyway, I know loads of people and quite a few of them are single so you might meet someone new.'

'I don't want anyone new,' I say, pulling the fridge open and taking out the ham that I bought earlier. 'I'm fine on my own. Ham sandwich?' I ask, holding up the ham.

'Great,' he says, with a thumbs up and a grin. 'We'll resume this convo another day.'

'We won't,' I say, slapping a slice of bread on the worktop and buttering it. 'We definitely won't.'

Ben laughs. 'I'll get you your house warming present,' he clomps off down the hallway and I hear things crashing to the floor in the hallway as he unloads his holdall.

I'm stunned, a house warming present; I never get a birthday card let alone a present from him and my birthday's the same day as his.

He returns after a few moments and shoves a package wrapped in a carrier bag at me.

'I hope it's not broken,' he says. 'I forgot it was in the bag when I threw it on the floor.'

'Thank you,' I say, taking it from him and unwrapping it from the bag that's twisted around it. 'It's the thought that counts anyway.'

I pull the bag off to reveal a large china mug.

'It's ace, isn't it?' Ben grins. 'I had to buy it when I saw it.'

I turn the mug round by the handle and read the slogan underneath the picture of a house.

Happy new home! I hope your new neighbours aren't bastards.

* * *

'I suppose we'd better make a start,' Ben says, reluctantly.

We're sitting on the bench underneath the window having just eaten ham sandwiches – Ben had two rounds – and drunk two mugs of tea each. I'm glad now that I never bought the sun beds because I think we would have ended up lying on them for the afternoon instead of cutting the grass. I might get them next week when the garden's done; no point in having a big garden if I'm not going to make use of it.

'I thought you could do the grass with the new lawnmower I've bought and I'll do the edges with the strimmer thing.' I say.

'Sounds like a plan.' Ben says, as he studies Bert's garden.

'Lovely, isn't it?' I say.

'It is. Have you met the neighbours? They're not

bastards are they?' he laughs.

'Shh,' I say, quietly. 'Keep your voice down. The lovely garden is Bert's, and the other side is Diana's. I've met them both and they seem very nice.' I'm lying a bit about Diana but I can hardly say what I think in case she's out in her garden and she overhears me. At the mention of Bert's name I feel a pang of regret; I felt we were going to be firm friends despite our age difference but it seems that Bert has other ideas and I've misconstrued his friendliness.

'That's the good thing about a small town,' Ben says, with a sigh. 'I don't even know who lives next door to me in London. I could die alone in my flat and I'd lay undiscovered until you realised you hadn't heard from me.'

Something else I thought I'd never hear my brother say; he normally refers to our home town as full of nosy sods who can't mind their own business. Perhaps he's serious about moving out of London; it would be nice if he was closer to me and Mum. We sit in companionable silence and the distant drone of a lawnmower reminds me of childhood summers that seemed to last forever. My eyelids are starting to droop when Ben speaks.

'That's a hell of a fence on the other side. Even I can't see over it.' he says, studying Diana's seven foot high fence.

'I know,' I laugh. I nearly tell him that I'm glad it's so high but stop myself just in time, remembering that she could be listening.

'Will I have to creosote or stain it or whatever you have to do to fences in the future,' I ask Ben, nodding at the fence. 'Or will my neighbour have to do that?' Ben always seems to know these sorts of things even though he doesn't have a garden himself.

He looks at me with a quizzical look.

'You will, obviously.'

'I thought she might as it's her fence.'

'It's not her fence,' Ben says. 'It's yours.'

'Is it?'

'Yeah, it's on the left which is the general rule but the way it's put up confirms it – the good side is on your side which means it belongs to you. You'd hardly put the rough side facing your own garden, would you?'

'No, I suppose not,' I say.

'Looks brand new anyway,' says Ben. 'I shouldn't think it's been up for more than a few months.'

I silently thank the previous owner of my house; but for her I'm sure I wouldn't have been able to step out into my own back garden without Diana accosting me and making demands on my time. Her decision to move to Australia must have been made very quickly as putting a fence up like that wouldn't have been cheap. You'd hardly go to all that expense it you weren't expecting to get the benefit of it.

'You've gone quiet,' Ben says.

'Just thinking,' I reply.

'Care to share?'

'Not now,' I say, standing up. 'I'll tell you later.'

I was starting to feel a bit bad about Diana despite my list of resolutions for the new me. I was beginning to wonder if I was being unkind by refusing her offer of coffee, wondering if I'd misunderstood what she said about me doing her tax return for free. In other words, I was resorting to the old mouse-like me who was basically a push over. Now I know that the previous owner of my house might have felt the same way about Diana as I do, otherwise why put a high fence up? She didn't put one on Bert's side. I feel better about it and resolve to continue my polite cold shoulder treatment.

'Come on, *Benny*,' I say, knowing my brother hates being referred to by his full, Abba tribute name. 'Time to earn your dinner.'

'Okay *Anni-Frid.*' He stands up, stretches his arms above his head and yawns. 'Lead me to your lawn-mower.'

CHAPTER SEVEN

The chicken is roasting in the oven, the vegetables are prepped and ready to put on to boil and the dining table is set neatly with my new placemats and cutlery. I've completed the look by picking some wild flowers from the very end of the back garden and putting them in an old beetroot jar and placing it in the centre of the table. Ben says the wild flowers are actually weeds; he thinks that now he's cut the grass it makes him some sort of gardening expert but I'm not taking any notice of what he says. Anyway, they're colourful and look very pretty so I don't care.

Ben and I manhandled the table and chairs in from the garage to put in the dining room as I thought that we might as well use them until I up cycle them. They're in pretty good condition despite their age and are made from good quality, solid pine and the chairs are very sturdy. The wood has turned a deep ginger colour and I contemplate how I'm going to up-cycle them – do I paint them after I've rubbed them down and stripped off the ginger varnish or do I restore them to the original colour? I can't decide but there's no rush to make a decision as they can stay in the dining room until I'm ready to start work on them. They make the house seem cosier, somehow and less as if I've just moved in. I only got them in because I knew that Mum would be horrified if I asked her to eat her Sunday roast from her lap but now I'm glad that they're in here and not in the garage.

I turn the vegetables on to boil and then get the roasting tray out of the oven and turn the potatoes over. Mum will be arriving at any moment and for the hundredth time today, I contemplate what I'm going to tell her about my missing locket.

I can't find it; I've done a search of the entire house every day this week, praying that it will somehow magically appear and that I've missed it on my previous searches. I've mentally retraced my footsteps a thousand times and although common sense tells me otherwise, I'm still convinced that I took the locket off in the bathroom as usual and left it on the window sill. I couldn't have, of course, because if I did it would be there and I wouldn't have turned the house upside down looking for it. I was so convinced that I even pulled back the lino on the floor to make sure that it hadn't somehow fallen off the shelf and worked its way underneath.

Phoebe helped me to do a thorough search of the shop but even as we looked for it I knew that we wouldn't find it. Phoebe, bless her, laid on the floor in the aisles and swept underneath all of the shelving with a broom handle. Aside from dust bunnies and the odd sweet there was nothing under there. I think that realistically, the only thing that could have happened is that the chain broke and the locket fell and I lost it on my way to or from work. Or if it did happen in the shop then someone has picked it up and kept it, although I doubt that because I'm sure I would have noticed it fall. In my desperation to find it I've scanned the pavement each day on my way to and from work which is ridiculous as it wouldn't still be there after all this time.

If it was a standard locket it wouldn't be so bad because I could replace it and not tell Mum, but that's just not possible. The locket is irreplaceable; not only because of the sentimental value but because I don't think I'll ever find another one that looks exactly like it. It's a large silver oval with intricate engraving on both sides and the front of the locket has a ruby set into the very centre; totally unique as well as being an antique.

I'm going to have to lie, I decide, to give myself more time. Maybe if I scour the antique jewellery websites I can find something similar to it. I know that I'm just putting off the inevitable but I can't face telling her today, she's going to be devastated; I'm devastated. I feel sick that I've lost it because it meant so much to me but realistically, there's no way I'm going to find it now. I'm going to tell Mum that the chain snapped and it's at the jewellers being repaired while I try and source a replacement.

The doorbell rings to signal Mum's arrival and Ben thunders down the hallway to let her in. I hear squeals of excitement from Mum when Ben opens the door – we'd kept his visit a surprise for her – and a hundred questions from her to him.

'You kept that quiet!' she says, as she comes into the kitchen.

'He wanted to surprise you,' I say.

She walks over to me and kisses me on the cheek.

'Well it's a lovely surprise.' She hands me a bottle of wine. 'I bought this to go with lunch.'

I take it from her and put it in the fridge to chill next to the one that I bought on special offer from Tesco. I think we'll be drinking her rather expensive bottle instead of mine.

'Now then Benny.' Mum puts her arm around Ben and guides him into the lounge. 'Let's leave Anni-Frid to it and you can tell me all about it.'

'About what?' I hear Ben ask.

'Well about Monica, of course,' Mum says. 'I wasn't born yesterday you know, I can tell when there's something wrong with my boy.'

I smile to myself.

Ben never could get anything past Mum.

✳ ✳ ✳

'Well, darling, I have to say that was absolutely delicious.' Mum puts her knife and fork down neatly on her plate.

I think delicious might be pushing it but it was pretty good, the roast potatoes came out just perfect although I think that might have been more by accident than design. Clean plates all round though so not half bad.

'Yeah, was good, sis. Any of them potatoes left?' Ben asks.

'No, all gone, I'm afraid. I'll get the pudding when our dinner's gone down.'

'Oh, yes darling, let's have a breather first.' Mum takes a sip of her wine and looks around the dining room. 'This is a very good size room, you know. I didn't realise how big it was when you had no furniture in it.'

'Yes, it's not a bad size,' I agree. Thankfully, we've had the locket conversation and Mum fell for it when I told her it was being repaired. I'm keen to keep the conversation away from the subject as Mum has a keen eye for spotting when I'm lying and I'm likely to confess if she starts questioning me or looks at me for too long.

'You should think about moving back home,' Mum says, turning to Ben. 'You could buy yourself a house if you sold that flat. You wouldn't have to have a little terraced like this you know, you could have a nice big detached. I could help you look.' Ben ignores her and stares fixedly at his wine glass. Mum has been fully updated re the Monica situation and now operation 'bring Ben home' has commenced.

'Hey, don't diss my house,' I say, in an attempt to get her off the subject of Ben moving. 'It might be small but it's bought and paid for.'

'Oh, it came out all wrong, Anni-Frid, I'm so sorry, your house is adorable, of course.'

'Well, adorable might be stretching it,' I say.

'No, it is,' Mum protests. 'And an absolute bargain, too. You got this place so much cheaper than the normal market value of these houses.'

I'm surprised that Mum has remembered how much it was; I did tell her when I put the offer in but I honestly didn't think she'd take enough notice to remember.

'And do you know,' she says, as she picks up her wine glass. 'That the previous owner paid *more* than you did? Now *that's* what I call a bargain.'

I sneak a look at Ben; he's staring into the distance and I suddenly feel sorry for him. I well remember how devastated I was when I found out that Tom was cheating on me; Ben's now feeling just like I did and it's still so raw for him. He's been putting a brave face on but knowing how I felt, he'd rather run away and hide away somewhere alone until he's ready to face the world again.

'And how on earth would you know that, Mum?' I ask, determined to keep our conversation going so she'll keep from nagging Ben to move back home.

'Well I looked on Zoopla, of course. Haven't you

had a look?' she asks.

I stare at her, to say that I'm shocked that she's capable of searching for my house on the internet would be an understatement. Mum is far from stupid but has always been totally disinterested in the internet or *any of that modern nonsense* as she's always called it.

'You should have a look,' she continues when I don't answer. 'I can show you how if you don't know how to do it. It makes for very interesting reading. I was shocked at what some of my neighbours have paid for their apartments. Far more than me.'

'Of course I know how to,' I say. 'I'm just surprised that you do. No offense, Mum, but you have trouble using the TV remote control and the satnav.'

'Pah!' She waves a hand. 'Of course I know how to use the internet, there's no point in not knowing because you have to move with the times. Some of my friends refuse to learn and are quite proud about it, as if they're making a point but all they're doing is making life difficult for themselves. You probably don't remember but I took lessons last year. It wasn't long after you moved out and into that awful rented flat. I felt at a bit of a loose end after you'd gone and they had a course on at the college so I thought it was time that I caught up with the times. I may be sixty-eight but I'm not quite past it yet.'

I feel bad; Mum would have told me this before

but it never penetrated my coat of misery because I was so wrapped up in myself.

'Of course you're not past it, Mum,' I say. I never thought that Mum wasn't capable, I just didn't think she was interested. She's young for her age and she looks young, too. 'I think it's great that you're keeping up with new technology.'

'Oh, I am,' Mum says, proudly. 'I've got myself a very nice laptop too. You can do pretty much anything on-line, you know. It's been a god-send. Tricia who does my hair helped me set it up because she's had one for ages. You should get yourself one.'

I don't spoil her moment of glory by telling her that I've had one for years, if I hadn't been so selfish this past year I could have helped her set it up myself.

'Anyway,' she goes on. '*That's* how I know that you got this house ten thousand pounds cheaper than what the previous owner paid for it.'

'Yes but that's to be expected – she'd have paid over the odds,' I say. 'She bought it during the boom when house prices were at their highest and that's still going to be more than they'd sell for now.'

'No.' Mum shakes her head. 'That's not the case, she only bought it a year before you.'

'Really? God, I bet she's cheesed off, then,' I say, as I pile up the plates in readiness to carry them through to the kitchen. I don't want to take the wind out of Mum's sails but there's no way this house was sold just over a year ago. I distinctly remember that Jayne, the previous owner, said that she felt like she'd lived here forever. It stuck in my mind because getting conversation out of her was like getting blood out of a stone and the little bit that she volunteered stands out in my mind.

I go out to the kitchen and dump the plates in the sink. I put the oven gloves on and take the sticky toffee pudding out of the oven and place it on the top. There's enough pudding for six people but I know my brother would have no trouble demolishing the whole lot if I let him. I probably will let him; he never puts weight on so why not, it'll stop me eating the leftovers. It looks and smells pretty damn good, though I say so myself. I pull open the freezer and get the tub of ice cream out, my mouth watering at the prospect of all that sugar. I carry it through to the dining room and place it on the table with the scoop and then return to the kitchen to get the pudding.

'So,' Mum says, as she serves herself a miniscule portion of pudding with an even smaller portion of ice cream. 'Even if you decided to sell immediately you'd make a good profit.'

Mum looks so pleased with herself that I don't have the heart to spoil it for her and tell her that Jayne had lived here for years.

'I would,' I agree. 'Although I have no intention of moving. I'm here to stay.'

I am, I suddenly realise, although I've been here less than two weeks, it already feels like home.

I've definitely moved on.

CHAPTER EIGHT

This is only my second week, and my first Monday working in the mini-mart but it feels as if I've been here for much longer. Not in a bad way, either; I feel comfortable and at ease and Phoebe is so easy to get along with. Surprisingly, I've also found that I still like working with the public and the novelty hasn't worn off. Most of the customers that come into the shop are cheerful and chatty and the miserable ones, well, I can ignore them. After years of working in an office environment and seeing the same faces day in, day out, I've discovered that I'm not the introvert that I thought I was; I like talking to people. An office is a very insular working environment and it's clear to me now that a change is just what I needed.

Phoebe isn't the nervous workaholic that I first took her for – another rule to add to my list; stop making snap judgements and judging by appearances. Although haven't I just done that with

Diana? I have, and yet I have no intention of revising my opinion of her because sometimes first impressions are right.

So maybe I'll just give up on my list altogether as it's getting longer every day and honestly, I can't keep up with it.

Phoebe has a great sense of humour and even if we didn't work together, I think we would definitely have become friends if we'd met elsewhere. In the lull when there are no customers coming in – usually around nine-thirty and again at eleven-thirty – Phoebe brings me a mug of coffee and we have a chat which is getting longer and longer every day. I've told her all about what happened with Tom, which is unusual for me because I'm usually a very private person but instead of bottling everything up I thought, why not tell her? It doesn't have to be a secret because it's just a part of my life and anyway, I've moved on now. Tom is in the past – even if I'm not completely over him.

Phoebe is an enthusiastic member of a local drama group and has already tried to persuade me to join. My first instinct was absolutely not because I couldn't imagine I'd ever want to be on a stage and the focus of everyone's attention. Phoebe said to have a think about it because I wouldn't have to be *on* the stage. The group are always desperate for people to help out with painting the scenery and other stuff so I could do that. I will give it some serious thought and maybe I should consider joining in on the stage; maybe it's time to step out of my comfort zone a bit and do something new. She said that aside from the plays that they put on there's an active social life involved as they have regular nights out and day trips organised. She said there's a big mix of age and genders so it would be a good opportunity to make new friends. I've left my old friends in the past and realistically, that's where they'll be staying so I need to start a new life.

Very tempting but just not yet; I need to get properly settled before I make anymore changes to my new life so maybe in a couple of week's time. I can't cope with too many changes at once but the more I think about it, the more appealing the idea becomes.

✻ ✻ ✻

I come in from the garden, wash my hands and put the kettle on. I've had a very productive afternoon and I'm feeling rather pleased with myself. When I got home from my shift I had a quick sandwich and then took two of the pine dining chairs out into the garden. I spread an old sheet on the ground and proceeded to sandpaper all of the old varnish off them. It was such a lovely day that it seemed ridiculous to work in the confines of the garage when I could be outside enjoying the sunshine. The chairs look completely different now that the hideous ginger varnish has gone and I've decided that I'm not going to paint them after all.

I've put them in the garage for now but tomorrow I'll give them a good wash down with a gentle detergent and put them back in the dining room. By the time I'd finished the sandpapering the sun wasn't quite as warm as it had been and there was a definite chill in the air but I felt as if I'd achieved something. There was the added bonus that all the time I was doing it, I never once thought of Tom – which has to be a good thing. The downside was that I didn't see Bert at all; I thought he might have been out pottering around in his garden as it's such a lovely day but his back door stayed firmly closed. I've decided that I'm going to knock on his door on my way home from work tomorrow to check on him because I'm concerned about him. If Bert gives me the cold shoulder, so be it; I'm not going to allow that to stop me from making sure he's okay – he's not in the first flush of youth and I'd hate to think he'd been taken ill and wasn't able to tell anyone.

I make myself a mug of coffee and take it through to the lounge for a well-deserved sit down. It's nearly seven o'clock so it's going to be microwaved scrambled eggs on toast for dinner. This is one of the bonuses of being on my own; I can do exactly as I like – Tom would have been horrified at the thought of egg on toast for dinner as he would never have anything less than a 'proper' cooked meal of meat and two veg.

I've just swung my feet up onto the sofa and am about to turn the TV on when a flash of purple from the lounge window catches my eye. I squint at the window and watch with dismay as I see Diana opening my front gate and marching purposefully up the path towards my front door. I've barely had time to register the thought before the doorbell shrills; I feel suddenly depressed that the relaxing evening I was looking forward to is now doomed. I'm going to have to invite her in and put up with her over-bearing, bossy presence while fending off demands for free accountancy services.

When the doorbell rings impatiently again I quickly jump up from the sofa and scuttle out to the kitchen. I stand behind the open kitchen door which hides me should Diana decide to peer through the opaque glass into the hallway. The doorbell shrills yet again and this time Diana keeps her finger on it and the persistent ringing is enough to wake the dead. When the bell stops abruptly I slowly edge my head around the edge of the door and peer into the hallway to see if she's still there. I watch as a blur of purple through the opaque glass slowly moves backwards away from the door. I breathe a sigh of relief. Thankfully, the fact that I haven't answered the door has convinced her that I'm not in.

I turn and take a step into the lounge and then hurriedly step backwards into the kitchen again; Diana is standing outside my lounge window with her nose pressed up against the glass. Her hands are cupped around her eyes and she's peering in through the venetian blind slats. I'm not sure whether she can see into the lounge but after a few moments she steps away. I edge into the lounge and sidle along the wall to the window and peer sideways through the blinds. Diana is walking down the path and when she reaches the gate she flings it open with force and it hits the garden wall with a clang. The gate is left swinging as she walks along the front path to her own house.

I stand still, undecided what to do. I feel completely ridiculous for hiding from my next door neighbour in my own home.

Absolutely pathetic; that's what I am. My former mood of achievement has now vanished and I'm annoyed with myself for being so gutless that I've hidden from her rather than man up and answer the door. I could have easily made an excuse to her; I *should* have made an excuse because she'll only come back because that's the sort of person she is. Or I could simply have told the truth; I've had a busy day and I'm not up for company because there's no law that says I have to do as she wants.

And who on earth looks through someone's window to see if they're in when they can't get an answer at the door? Normal people would have taken the hint by now instead of insisting of pursuing someone who is obviously not interested in being friends with them. I need to put a stop to this because I've moved here to start a new life, not to spend all of my time hiding because I don't want to be best friends with my next door neighbour.

I close the blinds and go and sit back down on the sofa and pick my mug of coffee up; she probably knew I was in anyway because my car is parked outside the house. She may have even seen me outside in the garden all afternoon; she'd only have had to have looked out of her bedroom window to see me so pretending I'm not in was pretty pointless.

I curse myself for my cowardice and panicked hiding; this is not the way I want to behave. I'm now aware that I don't want to put the television on because she might hear it through the wall and then she'll know for sure that I was in. I don't *have* to answer the door when she calls, do I? Of course not; my brother would think it perfectly acceptable to ignore her and would find the fact that I hid from her hilarious. Mum would have simply opened the door and told her that she'd had a busy day and wasn't up to having company – all said very politely, of course. *That's* what I should have done – except I have a feeling that Diana would have bulldozed her way in here anyway because I'm too much of a wimp to stop her.

I sit on the sofa brooding for an hour and then make myself turn the television on. I have to give myself a good talking to stop myself from turning the sound down low. For all Diana knows I was in the bath and I didn't hear the doorbell.

I stare at the TV and brood.

Another item to add to my list; stop being such a bloody coward.

Scrap that; the list is so long now that I can't even remember what's on it.

* * *

I'm dreaming.

I'm marching around my old home and Tom is there with his secretary who for some reason doesn't look like his secretary at all but is the image of a soap actress from Eastenders whose name I don't know. Their new baby is not with them; they left him on a bus and are waiting for the conductor to bring him back although how I know this I have no idea. They are laughing hysterically at me as I'm concerned that they're not looking after their child properly and for some reason it's my duty to make sure that they're responsible parents. I dream all of this bizarreness in the few seconds before I wake up and realise that the laughing is not a dream but is, in fact, real.

I lie in the darkness and listen; I left the window ajar when I went to bed as this room can be stuffy and airless and although the sound is faint it's vaguely familiar and seems to be coming from outside. I peer at the illuminated numbers on the clock on the bedside table and see that it's past three o'clock in the morning – very late to be playing a car radio in the street.

As I lay listening I realise that it's not coming from the street at all but from the wall between my house and Diana's. The sound is fuzzy and I wonder if Diana's fallen asleep with the television on. I know that you can watch TV twenty-four hours a day if you want to; there is always something to watch on one of the millions of channels. I know this from bitter experience after Tom and I split up because I suffered with terrible insomnia and spent many a night watching old films and reruns of old series. I did this for quite a few months until I came to the conclusion that if I was going to be awake all night I might as well be productive. I moved from watching TV to ironing; my clothes had never been so well pressed before or since; even socks and knickers got flattened.

Chanting has replaced the ha-ha-ha-ing and a memory buried deep in my childhood gradually resurfaces. Dad had a huge collection of old LPs and singles and Sunday afternoons became music time, especially in the winter when it was too wet to play outside. I suddenly recognise the song, Ben and I always begged Dad to play it because we'd never heard anything like it and we didn't know whether to laugh or be afraid of the vaguely creepy lyrics. The song ends and I'm about to turn over to go back to sleep when it starts again. *They're coming to take me away, ha-ha, to the funny farm* starts to play and I lie in bed and listen to the words that I know off by heart. I'm considering banging on the wall to wake Diana when the music abruptly stops mid-song and the room falls silent. Diana must have woken up and turned it off, although why she would have it on repeat, God only knows. I turn over and snuggle down under the duvet to go back to sleep, aware that I've got work in the morning and don't really want to be lying awake all night. As I drift off a thought pops into my head and I attempt to dismiss it – I don't want any more weird dreams tonight.

But the thought refuses to budge and I go to sleep with it playing on my mind.

Why should an old song make me feel threatened?

CHAPTER NINE

It was busy in the mini market this morning – unusual for a Wednesday – so I don't have time to think too much about last night until I'm walking home.

It's all feeling very surreal now and I'm not completely sure that I didn't dream the whole thing. When I went to bed the whole *hiding from my neighbour thing* was playing on my mind so did I dream that I woke up and could hear music? Diana was on my mind even though I tried to pretend to myself that she wasn't; I spent the evening alternating between feeling bad and pathetic for hiding and feeling annoyed that she won't seem to take the hint and leave me alone.

Even if I wasn't dreaming and Diana had fallen asleep and left the television or radio on, why on earth would I feel in any way threatened by that? It certainly wasn't directed at me. I'm sure that my insomnia induced TV watching would have annoyed my previous neighbours if they'd heard it but it wasn't in any way intentional so I'm sure Diana's noise wasn't either.

By the time I've turned the corner into my street I resolve not to dwell on it and to get a grip, as my brother would say, and stop fixating on trivia. As I continue down the street I'm relieved to see that Bert is out in his front garden. He looks absolutely fine and is clipping the top of the hedge although it's already perfectly straight without a leaf out of place. As I get closer he spots me and stops what he's doing and comes over to the garden wall.

'Hell, Frida, lovely day for it,' he says, leaning on the top of the wall.

'It is. I can't believe it's been like this for over a week now.'

'Forecast says it's going to break at the weekend so we'd better make the most of it,' he says, with a grimace.

'That's a shame,' I say, with a smile. 'But not a surprise.'

'Thought I'd better get out and tidy this garden up,' he says, looking around him. 'It's got into a bit of a pickle these last few days.'

'Where?' I laugh, looking at his immaculate garden.

He chuckles. 'Well, you know, maybe I'm a bit over the top with it but I can't help myself. Keeps me out of mischief anyway.'

'It looks lovely and it always does. I've made a start on my back garden, my brother came for the weekend and we tidied it up a bit and it looks much nicer. I'll be getting out to do the front next, weather permitting, maybe I'll start tomorrow if the weather's going to break at the weekend.'

'Well, if you need any help, you know where I am.'

'Thanks, Bert.' I say. 'I'm off into town this afternoon, is there anything I can get you while I'm there?'

'Not that I can think of, but thank you for the offer.' Bert looks down at his hands for a moment. 'Look, I'm glad I've caught you, Frida, because I wanted to apologise.'

'Apologise?' I say, in surprise. 'What on earth for? You've done nothing to apologise for, Bert.'

'Oh, I have,' he says, shaking his head. 'I was rude to you the other day and I had no right. I was abrupt with you and it wasn't your fault. I'd had a bit of a falling out with my daughter, you see, and I'm afraid I took it out on you and I'm very sorry about that and I hope you'll forgive me.'

'Of course I will, although there's absolutely nothing to forgive,' I say, relieved that Bert wasn't giving me the cold shoulder after all.

'Thank you. I wish my daughter was as easy to apologise to.' Bert chuckles but looks sad at the same time.

'You've not made up?' I ask.

'Well, sort of, it's not her fault that she doesn't know what it's like to be old. I don't blame her, I was like that once. She'll understand when she gets to my age.'

'Well, if you want to talk about it, Bert, you know where I am.' I stop myself from asking him what's happened as I don't want to overstep the mark.

'Storm in a teacup,' he says. 'She's just upset because I'm not going to visit her even though I've explained why I can't be away for that long.'

I remember the conversation now; his daughter wants him to go to Australia for the summer and he won't leave his garden. I'm about to offer to look after it for him but stop myself; the last time I offered he got a bit funny about it.

'I'm sure it'll all blow over,' I say.

'I hope so,' he says, wistfully.

I feel sorry for him and I want to tell him to go, what does it matter about a garden, who cares if every single plant dies when you have the opportunity to see your daughter and grandchildren because who knows what the future holds, especially at Bert's age. It might be the last chance he gets to see them. I'm struggling to understand why he would let the state of his garden stop him, I know he likes it tidy but he doesn't strike me as the sort to be obsessed over something. Although he hasn't mentioned Barkley I wonder if that's the real reason he won't go because he can hardly take him to Australia. Maybe he's afraid to leave him in kennels for a long time. But he doesn't need to because if that's what's stopping him, I could look after him. I'm going to offer, I decide, because if that is what's stopping him from going I want him to know that I'd take good care of him. If I offend him so be it.

'Bert,' I start to say.

'Oh, that's my phone ringing,' he says, looking towards his house. 'I'll have to go and answer it but we'll chat later.'

I've barely time to say goodbye before he disappears into his house and closes the front door behind him.

Funny, though, because I never heard his phone ringing; he must have better hearing than me.

* * *

I've been in all three jewellery shops in the town and none of them have anything remotely resembling my locket. I'm not surprised, the shops are all too new and modern and part of big chains so unlikely to have anything different from the latest fashion. I'm now trekking through the precinct and crossing my fingers that the tatty old jewellers shop that has been in Jubilee Street since I was a child is still there. As well as new jewellery which they always somehow manage to make look old-fashioned, they also sell second-hand clocks and jewellery. It's my last hope and too late, I realise that it's a Wednesday afternoon, so if they're as old-fashioned as I remember then they're going to be closed. Did I subconsciously know this? Did I deliberately come here today so that I'd have to come back another day and could thereby put off for a bit longer telling Mum that I've lost the locket? Because I promised myself that if I can't find a locket replacement today I was going to go round straight her house on the way home from town and confess to her that I'd lost it.

I've also promised myself that I'm going to man up and unblock Tom's number so he can contact me instead of pestering Ben. I've been promising myself that since Monday but haven't actually done it yet; if I don't do it tonight I might as well forget my resolutions of being a new, assertive person and give in and resort to my old, pushover, wimp-ish, doormat, mousy self.

I turn the corner into Jubilee Street and my mental ramblings are brought to a halt when I see that the jewellers is in fact still there and joy of joys, it appears to be open.

I open the door and enter and an old-fashioned brass bell attached to the door clangs above my head to announce my arrival. Instead of the ancient, white-haired old man I remember from my youth, a much younger woman is standing behind the counter.

'Hello, can I help you?' she asks.

I smile and walk over to the counter and wonder why it is that she looks so familiar.

'Yes, I'm looking for a silver locket in a particular style and I was hoping that you might have something similar.' I pull out my phone and scroll through the photos until I find the one that I've saved. It's an old photo that I've zoomed in on and cropped until only the locket is visible.

'Something like this?' I hold the phone up in front of her and she peers at it and frowns.

'Hmm, from memory I don't think that we have but we have a tray of some second-hand ones out the back, there may possibly be something in there. I'll be back in a moment.'

I wait while she opens a door behind her and disappears through it. It's only when she reappears with a large velvet tray in her hand that it hits me who she is.

'Jayne!' I say. 'I've just realised who you are!'

She flushes scarlet from neck to forehead and places the tray on the counter without speaking. She then unclips the top of the tray to reveal rows of silver necklaces. She pushes the tray closer to me but doesn't speak.

I look at her but she's looking down at the tray and I wonder if she's heard me; or perhaps I'm mistaken and she's not the previous owner of my house.

'I thought you were moving to Australia,' I say, deciding that if she did hear me she can at least answer because the more I look at her, the more convinced I am that it's her.

She doesn't answer.

'Immediately,' I add, starting to feel slightly annoyed at her rudeness.

'Change of plan,' she mutters quietly, not tearing her gaze away from the tray of lockets.

I've clearly put my foot in it; perhaps she was

going with a boyfriend or partner and it's all off now. The awkward silence stretches and I say nothing while she spins the tray around for me to look at the various necklaces. I wish I hadn't opened my mouth now; especially when I remember how reticent she was when I viewed her house. Speaking is obviously a big effort for her and I feel sorry that she's so socially awkward but equally, why would you want to work in a shop if you can't bear speaking to people? I make a pretence of studying the lockets although I can see immediately that I've wasted my time.

'What about this one?' She holds up a delicate locket.

'No, it's a similar design but far too small, mine was much bigger.'

'I'm sorry but that's all we have,' she says, laying it back down on the tray.

'Thank you for looking.' I put my phone back in my handbag. 'I'll just have to confess to my mother that I've lost it,' I say with a rueful smile. She stares at me blankly.

'Have you settled in alright?' She suddenly blurts out.

'Yes, fine thank you,' I say, surprised that she's decided to acknowledge the fact that I bought her house from her after all. 'It's a lovely house, I love it.' I feel beyond awkward; she's probably wishing she'd never sold it to me at such a bargain price and here I am telling her how wonderful it is.

'Good.' She snaps the lid over the tray and picks

it up and holds it to her chest as if I might snatch it from her.

'Well, nice to see you again,' I say lamely as I turn to leave. 'Thanks for your help.'

I have my hand on the door handle when she calls out to me.

'Don't tell anyone.'

I turn and look at her in puzzlement.

'Pardon?'

'That I'm still here,' she says.

'But...'

'It's embarrassing,' she says. 'That I didn't go. I'd rather people didn't know I was still here.'

'Of course,' I say, cheerfully, easing myself through the door. 'My lips are sealed.'

And anyway, who on earth would I tell?

I think Jayne is what Mum would call, in her old-fashioned way, *a bit special*.

Once outside I march briskly towards the multistory car park and muse over my conversation with Jayne. Very odd.

And I thought I had problems.

CHAPTER TEN

As predicted, the good weather broke last night and I woke this morning to the sound of heavy rain pounding against the bedroom windows. In typical fashion, the weather has decided to be vile just in time for the weekend.

I didn't sleep very well last night and had fitful dreams of moving my furniture around and it not fitting in anywhere because everywhere I turned there were boxes in the way. I kept dropping the boxes, making loud banging noises as I did so. The banging in my dreams must have been the thunder because that's what eventually woke me in the early hours of the morning. I lay awake for what seemed like ages watching the lightening flash around the room, counting the seconds between the strikes and bangs as the storm gradually moved further away.

Although I know that even if it hadn't been for the storm I wouldn't have slept.

And the reason I couldn't sleep is that Tom is

coming round to see me today.

In the true spirit of stopping being a wimp and trying to face up to things, I decided to take action. As soon as I arrived home from town after my fruitless search for a replacement locket, I texted Mum to say I'd pop over and see her this weekend. I should have gone straight round there from town, but quite honestly, I couldn't face it so I put it off. While I had the phone in my hand I also unblocked Tom's number from my phone. I then went a step further; knowing that he'd contacted Ben because he couldn't get hold of me I thought it unlikely that he would text me again so the best thing to do was to text him and ask him what it was he wanted. This took me an hour of typing a message, deleting it and then rewording it. The text that I eventually sent was exactly the same as the first one I typed. He replied almost immediately with *I need to talk to you* and a request for my address. I then texted back to ask what it was about but he wouldn't be drawn, just repeated that he needed to speak to me in person.

After stewing this over for another hour I decided to do the opposite of what I normally do – which is obsess over things endlessly and drive myself mad – but would speak to someone and actually talk about what might be the best thing to do. So, I rang Phoebe.

Phoebe shocked me by suggesting that the reason he's trying to contact me is that he wants me back. No way, I said; we're divorced and very much over. Doesn't sound like it, Phoebe said, because what other reason could there be? I had a good think and I couldn't think of any reason at all. She suggested I log back into Facebook and see if he's still with the secretary because that would confirm his intentions either way. I thought about having a look but I didn't feel at all comfortable about it; it would almost feel like stalking and I don't want to start doing stuff like that because who knows where it will end. I told Phoebe that I think she's most definitely wrong because there's no way I can imagine Tom wanting me back after everything that's happened. I haven't seen him since the day I walked out and despite his first feeble attempts to contact me and justify himself I've heard nothing from him.

When Phoebe suggested that Tom wants me back a feeling of hope surged through me and I attempted to push it firmly back down. I'm *almost* over Tom now and I don't want to go back there and stir it all up again.

But then the more I've thought about it the more I'm beginning to wonder if she might be right. Why else would he want to come round? We're no longer connected in any way, financially or otherwise so realistically, there's no reason for us to ever see each other again.

If he did want me back, would I want him? Honestly, I don't know. Of course I miss him and a part of me still loves him but I don't know if I could ever forgive the betrayal. Even if I could get past that, could I ever trust him again?

After we'd finished talking I took Phoebe's advice and texted Tom back with my address.

He's arriving in an hour.

I'll find out then exactly what he wants but before that I have an important decision to make.

What am I going to wear.

* * *

After much deliberation I settled on jeans and a pretty pink fitted T-shirt. I don't want it to look to Tom as if I've made an effort or that I care what I look like but equally, I don't want to look like a tramp who lives in her pyjamas all day. It's a very fine line; I stopped short of putting make up on and stuck to my usual tinted moisturiser and tinted lip balm. I wear this every day so I am definitely not making an extra effort, I'm just doing what I normally do.

I know I look decent; even though I stopped my obsessive *I must go to the gym every single day or I'll explode regime* the very minute I left Tom. I've actually lost weight without really trying as wherever possible I walk everywhere instead of driving. Also, because I'm not working in an office anymore I'm spared the constant temptation of biscuits and chocolate that one or other of my colleagues were always bringing in *as a treat* to counteract the boredom of office routine.

Not that I care one jot what Tom thinks, but I

have my pride.

Yeah, whatever, Anni-Frid, you're not fooling me, the real me sneers.

Thankfully, further ruminating is stopped as the doorbell shrills; he's arrived. I take a deep breath, go out into the hallway and open the front door.

Annoyingly, he looks as good as ever; fit and tanned from the recent sunshine and smiling that sweet smile that used to melt my heart. It's a shock to see him again after so long and out of nowhere a sudden urge to cry overwhelms me.

'Hi,' he says, quietly.

'Hi,' I manage to reply, my voice shaky.

Determined not to crumble in front of him I fight down my feelings, paste a smile on my face and invite him in. I walk down the hallway and into the lounge and he follows behind me and I use those few seconds to compose myself.

'Have a seat.' I gesture towards the sofa on the other side of the room as I perch myself on the sofa opposite him. He sits down and we face each other. I'd already made the decision not to offer him a drink before he arrived; I don't want to be too friendly or welcoming because, actually, he doesn't deserve it.

'Thanks for letting me come round,' he says, as he sits himself down.

I shrug, not trusting myself to speak.

'I've been trying to contact you for ages. When you blocked my calls I begged Ben to tell me where you'd moved to but he wouldn't. He told me I was a prick.' He laughs self depreciatingly. 'I can't blame him for that, I behaved like a complete arse.'

'That's the only reason I unblocked you, so you'd stop texting him,' I say. 'It didn't seem fair to drag him into it.'

'Well, thank you, I know it can't have been easy for you.' He looks around the lounge. 'Nice place you've got here, you must be pleased with it.'

'I like it,' I say, managing to sound defensive.

He gives me the old look, the one where he really *looks* at me and I feel myself start to blush and squirm under his scrutiny.

'You're looking good, Frida, that colour always did suit you.' He smiles and despite myself I feel pleased that he's noticed. I look down at the carpet and wonder what he's going to say next.

'I bumped into your old manager at Bowden's a while back. I was surprised when she said you'd left, I thought you were a lifer.' He laughs and I suddenly hate him for being so sure of himself that he thinks that he can walk in here after a year and behave as if nothing has happened and even make a *joke*. How dare he.

'Well, you know, some things have just had their day and you're just sick to death of them so it's time to move on,' I say quietly. I can't help feeling pleased when I see Tom wince. He's not sure if I'm getting at him. I'm not sure if I'm getting at him.

'So where are you working now?' he asks.

'In a mini market. Four mornings a week.' I

enjoy the look of surprise on his face.

'On the till,' I add.

'Brilliant,' he says, as if I've just told him I'm the managing director of Amazon. 'And how's your mum? Is she well? Still organising all of her friend's lives?' he asks, referring to our old in-joke about Mum.

'Yes she's fine,' I snap. 'And she has been for the last year, thanks for asking.'

'I did ask your brother if she was okay,' Tom says. 'I would have asked you but you blocked me.'

I glare at him; furious that he's trying to make me sound unreasonable for not wanting my cheating ex-husband to contact me.

'Okay, Tom, I'm assuming you didn't come round here to talk about my mum so what exactly do you want?'

Toms pulls a face and hold his hands up with a smile.

'Whoa, you don't take any prisoners, do you?'

'I'm waiting,' I snap. 'Tell me why you're here.' If he does want me back then he can bloody work for it; he needn't think he's going to waltz back into my life *that* easily.

Because the truth hit me the minute I opened the door and saw him standing there; I am going to take him back because I love him and I'll forgive him *anything*. Even a ten year long affair with another woman who's had his baby.

'Frida.' He stares at me and I can't look away. 'What I really came here for is to say that I'm sorry, so, so sorry. What I did was unforgiveable and believe me, I've hated myself every single day for what I did to you. I know that I have no right but I'm hoping that in time you'll find it in your heart to forgive me.'

I stare at him.

'If I could turn back the clock,' he continues. 'I would, there's absolutely no doubt about it.'

I hold my breath, aware of what his next words will be and my stomach flips over with excitement. I'm going to forgive him but I'm going to make him wait, I decide. I'm going to tell him that I need time to think about it because he needs to suffer a bit, too. Obviously it won't be anything like the hurt he's caused me but a few days of not knowing whether I'll take him back or not is definitely in order.

'And the thing is,' he continues. 'Even though it's over between us I sincerely hope that one day we can be friends again because I've missed your friendship.'

I gawp at him, not quite sure I heard him properly.

'What?' I gasp.

'I know you don't believe it now, but time does heal.'

I stare at him in disbelief and wonder how I could have got it all so stupidly wrong. If he doesn't want me back why is he even here?

'And in the spirit of moving on with our lives,' he says, seeming to read my mind. 'I was wondering if you still have my mother's engagement ring?'

'Your mother's engagement ring?' I echo.

'Yes.'

I do have it; it's upstairs in my dresser drawer in the same envelope as my Decree Absolute. I intended returning it to him one day but wasn't sure how to do that without seeing him.

'Of course I still have it,' I manage to mumble. 'I'd hardly throw it away.'

'Great. I knew you'd look after it. Do you think I could have it back? The thing is, Gem and I are getting married and it's only right that she has mum's ring now.'

I frown.

'What?' he asks.

And that's when I lost it.

Completely.

CHAPTER ELEVEN

I visited Mum today and confessed to her that I'd lost my locket; she was very upset, as I knew she would be, but she didn't lay the guilt on me because she could see how upset I was about it. We talked about where I might have lost it and she's offered to help me search my house again when she next comes over. She says sometimes a fresh pair of eyes can help. There's no way that it's anywhere in my house but I'm going to let her help me look again because at least it'll feel as if we're doing something.

We've just eaten a lovely beef roast that Mum cooked to perfection and she's now clearing up in the kitchen and won't let me help her, even though I offered. She's insisted that I put my feet up and relax while she loads the dishwasher.

I haven't told her about Tom's visit yesterday; I

will tell her but just not yet. I'm still processing what happened.

I feel like a complete fool; what the hell made me think that he wanted me back? I only hope that he didn't guess as much from my behaviour; I'm disgusted with myself at how easily I was prepared to forgive him. I've been fooling myself that I'd moved on and that somehow I've changed and am no longer the pushover that I used to be. That somehow, because I had a list of things in my head that I wanted to change about myself it meant that I *had* changed, that by not having coffee with an over-bearing neighbour I was a different, braver person.

I'm not; I'm the same pushover that I always was; the sort of person who's ready to forgive a cheating ex who's treated me like dirt. The sort of person who hides in her own home rather than answer the door to her obnoxious neighbour.

I'm feeling pretty sickened with myself although I'm trying very hard *not* to feel that way. I need to use this *Tom episode* as an example of how *not* to resort to my old ways. I need to not dwell on it but move on and make *real* changes. Yesterday was a wake-up call for me and I've realised that just having a list in my head is not going to make change happen; becoming the person I want to be is going to be an on-going process. I've gone right back to square one with one fleeting visit from Tom. When I think back to his comment of *time heals* I cringe; the absolute arrogance of the man.

The only comfort is that I gave full vent to my feelings with him – and even if *I* think I'm still a wimpy people pleaser, he definitely does not.

Despite moving on and buying my house and getting a completely different job, there was always a tiny part of me that wanted things back to how they were but I never admitted that to myself. I don't like change and that's a fact; I like things to stay the way they are and be comfortable. I now know that Tom and I will never get back together and even if we had, it wouldn't have worked. He's not the man I thought he was, or wanted him to be. I put him on a pedestal and never really saw him for what he was but I'm starting to now. He's not a bad man but he's weak; only a weak person could be so duplicitous. I may be a people pleaser and a bit of a pushover but actually, I don't think I'm weak because if I was I would never left Tom in the first place.

After Tom asked for his mother's engagement ring back, I stared at him in disbelief and realised that all of the apologising wasn't because he wanted me back but because he wanted something.

'We're done here,' I said, in a voice that didn't sound like mine at all. 'So you can get out of my fucking house.'

'Now,' I added menacingly. He gawped at me with his mouth hanging open and his eyes agog. I never usually swear and I could see the shock in his eyes.

I rather liked it.

'The ring?' he persisted in a quiet voice.

That's when I jumped up from the sofa, grabbed his arms and yanked him up out of the chair. Somehow, despite Tom being much bigger than me, I managed to manhandle and push him out into the hallway, open the front door and push him out onto the path. He turned around and stood there staring at me and I fought down the urge to hit him and wipe the superior expression from his face.

'You need to calm down,' he said with the faintest hint of a smirk.

'I'm quite calm,' I managed to say without shouting. 'But just for future reference, telling someone to calm down never works so next time you find yourself in a *situation* you might just want to SHUT. THE. FUCK. UP.'

'Okay, okay.' He held his hands up in a pacifying gesture. 'Look, if you want to keep the ring...'

'I don't want the ring,' I said, and I did shout this time. 'You can have it back when I get around to it. Or when I feel like it. Or maybe never, who knows? Maybe I'll give it to charity or flush it down the toilet or throw it in the river. I'll have a think about it but don't come round here pretending you're sorry and wanting to be friends when really, as usual, you just want something.'

'I am sorry.' He looked sad when he said it and for a moment I was *almost* fooled and then I remembered what a good actor he is.

'No you're not,' I said. 'You're a lying, cheating, conceited scumbag. People who are sorry don't lie to their wives for ten years and have the nerve to come round here asking for their mother's engagement ring. And as for the poor cow who's going to marry you, tell her from me that she's welcome to you because you're an arsehole. Goodbye.'

With that I slammed the door in his face. Seconds later I opened it again and he was still standing there in the same position.

'And don't text me. Ever. You're blocked,' I shouted at him.

I slammed the door again, turned around and stomped straight up the stairs and into my bedroom. I stood at the side of my bedroom window and watched as he slowly walked down the path to his car, got in and drove away. I couldn't see any neighbours out in the garden so I don't think there were any witnesses to it all but I actually didn't care, not one little bit.

I enjoyed it.

* * *

Still feeling stuffed with Mum's roast beef I pull up outside my house and park the car. Despite my confession about my locket, we had a lovely afternoon chatting about nothing in particular and watching bits of TV and Mum filled me in on the distant cousins and aunts and uncles latest gossip. I had to force myself to get in the car and come home as I could easily have stayed all evening and fallen asleep in the chair. Mum offered to put me up for the night but of course I have work in the morning. Although I didn't tell her about Tom somehow I'm already feeling better about it all.

I clamber out of the car and lock it; the lovely May sunshine that we'd enjoyed for over a week has completely disappeared and we're now back to constant rain and a temperature that feels distinctly winter-like. In a fit of optimism, I foolishly didn't take a jacket or a jumper with me and my long sleeved T-shirt is giving little protection against the chilly evening air. I'm scuttling towards my garden gate, arms wrapped around my body when I'm halted by the sound of Diana's voice.

'Been somewhere nice?'

My hearts sinks as I turn around to face her. She's standing on the path outside her own gate and I'm not sure if she's just arrived or leaving. Maybe leaving, because I'm sure I'd have noticed if she was in her car because it's parked right in front of mine. The thought pops into my head that she's been watching out of her window and waiting for me. I dismiss the thought; I'm not that important, she's not that desperate to befriend me. Besides, she looks dressed for a wedding and is wearing a smart cream dress with a floaty pink chiffon scarf arranged around her neck.

'Visiting my mother,' I say, with a totally fake smile. 'But I didn't realise how cold it was! I should have taken a jacket with me.' I rub my arms briskly, hoping that she'll take the hint that I want to get inside the house and not stand outside chatting to her.

'You're very lucky to have a mother to visit,' she says. 'My mother passed away last year and I miss her every day.'

'Oh, that's so sad. I'm sorry for your loss.' I'm not sure if it's appropriate to say that after so long, but I've said it now.

'Thank you.' She stands still and I wonder how I'm going to end this conversation and get away from her and then immediately feel bad – because she's just told me she lost her mother. How heartless am I?

'Have you been somewhere nice?' I ask, deciding that just because I don't want to be friends with her doesn't mean I can't be nice to her. She's obviously dressed up for something

'Not really,' she says, flatly. 'Now, when are we going to get together and have that coffee? My tax return really needs looking at.'

I stare at her.

'But surely your tax return isn't due until next year, now,' I say. 'It's only May.' I wonder why I'm letting myself get drawn into a conversation about her tax affairs; I am *not* doing it for her.

'Yes but I need to set everything up in advance, that's what my old accountant used to do.'

'I'm sorry,' I say, in what I hope is a firm voice. 'But I don't do accountancy anymore. You need to find someone else.'

'Tuesday evening,' she announces, as if I haven't spoken. 'I'm free on Tuesday evening. Come at six thirty and we'll make a start on it. Maybe you could bring your laptop too, it might be easier than using my old thing, I've had it for years.'

I'm speechless; why would she assume that I have a laptop and would want to bring it to do her tax return? The cheek of the woman defies belief. What do I say? How do I get out of this? She's determined to steamroll me into doing what she wants. I remind myself that I don't have to explain myself to her, she's just a neighbour and a pretty obnoxious and pushy one at that. All my previous sympathy for her dead mother disappears.

'I'm afraid I can't,' I say. 'I'm busy.'

'Doing what?' she demands.

'Stuff,' I say bluntly. If she doesn't take the hint from that then she never will. Part of me feels bad for sounding so rude but honestly, how brusque do I have to be before she gets the message?

She doesn't speak but steps forwards and looms over me, getting so close that I can smell her overpowering, cloying, perfume.

'Okay,' she says, thoughtfully as she puts her hand to her throat and loosens her chiffon scarf and pulls it away from her neck. 'We'll talk about it another time.' With that she abruptly spins around on her heel and marches back towards her front gate, pulls it open and walks up the path to her front door and lets herself in.

I stand immobile and stare at her house and try to make sense of what I've just seen, wondering if, somehow, I'm hallucinating.

Because when Diana pulled her scarf aside I saw something impossible, something that I've been searching high and low for and thought was lost forever.

She was wearing my locket.

CHAPTER TWELVE

'**A**re you absolutely sure it was your locket?' Phoebe asks.

'Absolutely,' I say. 'And it felt as if she was deliberately making sure that I saw it.'

Phoebe cocks her head to one side and smiles.

'Or maybe you don't like her and imagined that bit? Because she must have found it in the street but there's no way that she could know the locket was yours, is there?'

'That's true,' I laugh. 'Is it that obvious that I don't like her?'

'A bit, although from what you've told me she doesn't sound very likeable. Are you sure it's yours, it couldn't just be something a bit like it? If you only saw it for a few seconds maybe your brain saw a locket and filled in the details for you.'

'No, it's definitely mine,' I say. 'I know it.'

'So you got a really good look at it?'

'Well…no, but it's a very distinctive locket, there isn't another like it.'

'Okay.' Phoebe thinks about it for a moment. 'So when you ask her for it back you have to remember that even if it is your necklace she would have found it in the street where you lost it. You need to make sure that you don't sound as if you're accusing her of something. I mean it's not as if she stole it from you.'

Of course Phoebe's right. The locket must have fallen in the street going to or from somewhere and Diana simply picked it up. All I have to do is explain this to her and ask for it back.

'I'll ask her,' I say, with more confidence than I feel. 'Nicely. I'm sure she'll understand and it won't be a problem. If I found something and someone asked for it back I'd be fine about it. I have a picture of me wearing it so she'll be able to see that it's mine.'

''Of course it won't be a problem,' Phoebe agrees, as we walk over to the mini market doors. 'Just don't get so overcome with gratitude that you let her talk you into doing her tax return.'

'No chance!'

I'm thrilled that I'm going to get my locket back but why did it have to be Diana that found it? It's just my luck; I was trying my best to avoid having to talk to her if at all possible but now I'm going to have to. Although on the up side, Mum will also be delighted.

'We'll close up now,' Phoebe says. 'It's not quite half-past twelve but no one's been in for the last half an hour so I can't see the point of staying open any longer.'

It's bank holiday Monday and Phoebe only opens the mini market for the morning on bank holidays; she says it's not worth paying the staff double time for the day when she doesn't make any more money than a normal Monday. There was a morning rush at about ten o'clock when the locals came in for their newspapers and cigarettes but the shop has been quieter than the grave ever since; quieter than a normal Monday morning, actually.

'I'll pick you up about half one-ish?' Phoebe asks.

'Perfect. I'll be ready. I just hope the weather holds.' I cross my fingers and hold them up in the air as Phoebe holds the door open for me. I step outside into weak May sunshine.

'As long as it doesn't rain,' I say, gazing up at the clouds scudding across the blue sky. 'That'll do me.'

'Me too.' Phoebe gives me a wave and pulls the door closed and I set off at a brisk pace for the walk home. The sun is shining and although it's not as warm as it was before the weather broke on Friday night the fact that it's not raining is pretty amazing for a bank holiday. There's a bit of a spring in my step and it's not just because of the weather and the fact that I'm getting my locket back; no, I'm feeling rather pleased with myself because last night I did something extremely brave; well, for me anyway.

I opened up the Facebook app on my phone and looked at Tom's profile.

I didn't even have to search for him as he came straight up on my news feed because he's posted so many pictures of his son. I did feel a pang when I saw his beautiful baby and the secretary and him looking so happy. The secretary looked very glamorous in every single picture and as skinny as a rake and not like a new mum at all. As I looked at the pictures of her I waited for a feeling of hatred to wash over me but it didn't; I found that I could look at her quite dispassionately. As I forced myself to look at every single photograph I realised that it wasn't as bad as I thought it would be. I felt a bit sad but certainly not heartbroken; I think that I'm finally, *almost*, over Tom. Maybe it would have been different if I'd longed for a baby but I never have so that part didn't upset me at all. What did seem strange was that in some of the pictures I could see that they were still living in mine and Tom's old house with our old furniture; they even had the same covers on the sofa cushions. I don't think I'd like that if I was the secretary but realistically, without my wage Tom will be struggling to pay the mortgage.

I turn the corner into my street and walk briskly towards my house. I'll have a quick sandwich when I get in, get changed into something more summery and should still be ready for my half past one pick up. Phoebe and I are going to the summer fare that's on in the centre of town today. It's basically an outdoor market with lots of food and craft stalls with the local dance schools putting on a bit of entertainment. I'm really looking forward to it because it's a long time since I've been out or had anything like a social life.

As I reach my gate I glance over at Diana's house to see that her car is parked out the front; she's in. Should I knock on her door now and ask her about the locket? I could ask her and get it out of the way right this minute. I consider doing this for all of a nanosecond before dismissing the idea; it'll be a too much of a rush. I can hardly ask her about the necklace, get it back off her and then clear off. I'll feel obliged to make some sort of small talk otherwise I'll seem rude and mercenary. Who knows how long that would take and then time could be tight to get myself some lunch, get changed and be ready for Phoebe picking me up in three quarters of an hour.

I push the gate open and march up the path to my front door and even as I do it I know; I'm lying to myself and just putting off asking her because I just don't want to speak to her.

* * *

I jump out of Phoebe's car and she zooms off down the road with a wave and a toot of the horn. We've had such a great afternoon wandering around the stalls and chatting – I can't remember when I last enjoyed myself so much. When Tom and I were to-gether we wouldn't have even considered going to the town fayre because we'd have considered that a waste of a precious day off. Weekends were mostly taken up with doing all the stuff that we couldn't fit in during the week and of course, the gym abso-lutely had to be factored in so that we didn't both explode into fatness. I wonder if he still goes every-day; looking at the slimness of him I'm guessing that he does. I actually hate going to the gym now that I look back on it and I marvel at the fact that I forced myself to go every single day.

What a waste of time.

Phoebe and I finished off our day by having dinner at one of the pubs on the high street in-stead of coming home and cooking. We went for the early bird special at five o'clock as we thought it would be quieter; unfortunately everyone else had the same idea. We had to wait for our order but I didn't mind because it's not as if I needed to get home at a certain time. I've rarely been out so-cially since I left Tom and I'd forgotten how nice it is so I'll definitely be doing it more often. Phoebe is great company and it seemed that we couldn't walk more than a few paces without seeing some-one she knows and stopping for a chat. I'm going to join the drama club that she goes to, whether it's for scenery painting or acting, because I think it'll be fun and I need to get out there and make more new friends.

The sun is low in the sky and I check my watch

to see that it's nearly eight o'clock. Not too late to call on Diana and ask her about my locket, I decide, and I walk purposefully along the path to her house before I can change my mind. My rush of confidence is due in no small part to the two glasses of wine that I drank with my lasagne and salad.

I stand outside her front door, take a deep breath and rap the brass knocker smartly. Diana's house is very well kept; every windowsill is pristine white with not one speck of dirt on and her front door is painted a glossy black. Her garden is a mirror image of Bert's except that instead of rose beds she has assorted colourful flowers that I have no idea of the names of. Unless it's a daffodil or a rose, flowers are a mystery to me. Perhaps I should educate myself on all things garden and maybe even make a hobby out of it because I have plenty of free time now.

The door opens and Diana looks down at me and I smile my friendliest smile.

'Hi,' I chirrup. 'Have you had a nice day?'

'Not too bad, I suppose.' Diana doesn't look too thrilled to see me and I wonder if I'm in the dog house over my unwillingness to do her tax return. Or maybe I've interrupted her favourite television programme.

'At least it's not rained despite it being a bank holiday,' I say in a jolly fashion but Diana doesn't crack a smile. I take a deep breath and decide to just get it over with. 'The reason I've called round,

Diana, is that I wanted to talk to you about the locket you were wearing yesterday.'

'Locket?' Her brow furrows and she looks down at me with a puzzled expression.

'Yes.' I take another deep breath. 'The thing is, Diana, I lost that locket over a week ago and obviously you found it. Which I'm very pleased about as it has great sentimental value to me.' The words come out in a rush and I'm aware I'm gabbling but I can't seem to stop.

Diana stares at me blankly.

'What I'm trying to say is that I'd like it back, please,' I blurt. 'Because as I said it does have tremendous sentimental value because my father gave it to me so it means an awful lot to me.'

Diana continues to stare and the silence stretches uncomfortably. After what seems like forever, she finally breaks the silence.

'I'm sorry, Frida, but I have no idea what you're talking about.'

I'm not surprised; instead of the calm, casual conversation I'd envisaged, I've blurted it all out in a garbled mess so it's no wonder she's confused.

'Sorry, I've probably confused you,' I say, with a smile. 'The locket you were wearing yesterday – the large silver one with a ruby in the middle of it? Well, it's mine. I lost it...' Diana holds her hand up and I trail off mid sentence.

'It's okay, Frida, there's no need for you to repeat yourself, it's not that I didn't hear you but I have no idea what you're talking about. I don't *have* a locket.'

'You were wearing it yesterday,' I say.

'No.' She shakes her head. 'I'm afraid you're thinking of someone else. I wouldn't wear such a thing as a locket, especially a silver one. I'm allergic to cheap metals like silver you see; I only *ever* wear gold.'

I stand with my mouth hanging open while she holds my gaze with her pale grey eyes. Did I imagine she was wearing it? I doubt myself for a moment but quickly dispel that thought. Diana's lying; she has my locket, I know it.

But what can I say?

I can hardly call her a liar.

CHAPTER
THIRTEEN

T
he bleep of the alarm wakes me and I can't believe that it's time to get up already. I try unsuccessfully to focus on the numbers of the clock even though I know that as the alarm has gone off it means that it's six-thirty in the morning.

For the last three nights I've slept like the dead and have hardly been able to drag myself out of bed in the morning. Last night I dreamed that there was loud music playing and I needed to get out of bed to turn it off but I couldn't make my body move. My limbs were paralysed and I had to lie in the dark and listen to the thump-thump-thump of the music, although what the music was, I have no idea. I don't usually dream very much but lately I seem to dream all of the time.

I fool myself that I've been under the weather

and picked up some sort of bug over the last few days and that's why I feel so crap but I'm only lying to myself. I know that the truth is that my body is still recovering from the lack of any sleep on Monday night. After asking Diana about my locket, I couldn't settle and spent the night replaying the conversation over and over in my mind, thinking that somehow I'd misunderstood what she said. Perhaps I was seeing things and imagined the locket, because why on earth would she lie? I *must* have been mistaken, whatever she was wearing around her neck, it couldn't have been my missing locket. I tossed and turned all night with my thoughts playing on a loop and despite being exhausted the next day I was glad to actually get up and give up the pretence of trying to sleep.

I've spoken to Phoebe about it and between us we couldn't think of any reason for Diana lying. Even if she was annoyed with me for not wanting to do her tax return for her she'd hardly tell me a bare-faced lie just to get her own back. Normal people don't do that sort of thing. Besides, I think that Diana is the sort who always gets her own way in the end by simply not taking no for an answer. She's a very confident person and I would imagine that most people give in to her demands because they become exhausted with telling her *no*.

After she'd told me that she never had my locket I stood there gawping at her and as I turned to leave she asked me when I was coming round for a coffee. Not something that someone who's just lied to you and has a stolen locket in their possession would do, is it? I mumbled that I'd let her know and scuttled back down her path and along to my own house.

I'm not going to mention it to Phoebe again as I have the feeling that she thinks I'm a bit obsessed about it; not that she's said anything but I'm sure there was the faintest hint of a sigh when I brought the subject up again yesterday. She's also suggested on more than one occasion that maybe I'm mistaken about it. And even if I'm not, she says, what can I do about it?

Absolutely nothing.

Perhaps I have been going on about it a bit too much and got a bit fixated about it. I need to remember that even though Phoebe and I get along really well it's a very new friendship and there are certain boundaries; it's not as if I've known her for years. I don't want to spoil a blossoming friendship by making her think that I'm some sort of neurotic who can't let things go.

And the more I think about it, the more convinced I become that I'm the one who's wrong. It's not a good feeling because here I was congratulating myself on my new life and the new me but in reality I've imagined that my locket is hanging around someone else's neck. I feel embarrassed that I even asked her about it now; thank God that I was polite about it and didn't pursue the matter after she said she didn't have it.

I need to put the locket thing behind me; it's

gone and that's all there is to it. At least I've broken the bad news to Mum now and she's okay about it; I need to move on and let it go.

But I'm definitely not doing Diana's tax return.

I drag myself out of my nice warm bed and trudge towards the bathroom.

A good hot shower will sort me out.

* * *

A busy morning in the mini market and a couple of paracetamol and by the time I walk home after my shift I feel a lot better; not great but better than I did. I made sure not to whinge on to Phoebe about Diana or the locket and kept the conversation upbeat and cheerful. I even agreed to join her next week when she goes to her drama group. Very brave of me, I thought.

After lunch I carry the final two dining chairs out of the dining room and into the garage where I set about them with sandpaper. It's not warm enough to do it outside and the dark clouds scudding across the sky threaten rain. The garage has good light from the large side window and with the radio playing hits from the eighties, I find myself humming along and I soon lose myself in the work. Before I know it several hours have gone by and the chairs are finished. I stand back and survey my handiwork and can't help feeling pleased with myself. There's only the table to do now – which will be much easier as it doesn't have fiddly spindle legs and carved seat backs. I may resort to using my electrical sander on the top to get a nice, even, finish although I'll have to do it in the dining room as there's no way I'll be able to get the table out to the garage myself. Ben helped me last time; actually, he pretty much carried the thing on his own so who am I kidding. I'll cover the dining room with a sheet and shut the door to the lounge and kitchen which will contain most of the mess. Not today though, that's a job for another day.

I carry the chairs back into the house, one at a time, and on my second journey I see Bert is at his kitchen window and I give him a cheery wave which he returns. Once indoors I place the chairs back in position around the table and imagine how good it's going to look once the table is done.

I go back out into the kitchen and pull the fridge open and am debating what to cook myself for dinner when the doorbell shrills making me jump out of my skin. I mentally add the purchase of a new doorbell to my list of things to buy. The doorbell grates; it's shrill and far too loud and could wake the dead and nearly gives me a heart attack every time it rings. I peer around the door of the kitchen into the hallway expecting to see Diana's outline through the opaque glass of the front door. My mind whirrs into action as I try to think of a suitable excuse as to why I can't have coffee with her.

It's not Diana at the door; the outline of the person is dark and tall and looks very much like a man in a suit. I walk down the hallway and as I get closer to the door I become convinced that it's Tom.

What the hell does he want?

His mother's ring, I suddenly remember. In my preoccupation with my locket I'd completely forgotten about the ring. The doorbell shrills again, long, loud and incessant because he's kept his finger on the button. Rage washes over me and I unlock the door and brutally yank it open.

Tom stares back at me unsmilingly. He's suited and booted so has obviously called in here on his way home from work.

'I'll send you the ring when I'm ready,' I say. 'Coming around here pestering me isn't going to make it happen any quicker so goodbye.' I start to push the door closed but Tom puts his foot in the way. I look down at his foot in disbelief and in a fit of anger I swing the door back into the hallway ready to slam it onto his foot if he doesn't remove it.

'You bitch,' he says, as I'm about to slam the door. His voice is low and calm – a sure sign that he's spitting mad; in the ten years that Tom and I were married I rarely saw him lose his temper. This is the calm before the storm; the pre-cursor to Tom erupting. I open my mouth but before I can speak Tom steps up onto the door threshold and roughly pushes the door open nearly knocking me off my feet. I stumble awkwardly backwards into the hallway, just managing to stop myself from overbalancing by steadying myself on the wall.

'Okay Tom,' I say calmly, although my heart is racing. 'You'd better tell me what the hell you think you're doing before I call the police.'

'Be my guest.' He looms over me. 'It'll save me the job because you're not getting away with this.'

'Getting away with what?' I shout.

He looks at me with something that looks very much like hatred. I'm tempted to get my phone and call his bluff because who does he think he is barging into my home like this? I stare at him for a moment and then change my mind and close the front door because there's no need for the whole street to hear whatever it is he's come round here for. I don't really want to have to call the police and start something that is going to end up causing a whole load of hassle. I remind myself that I've done nothing wrong and to not allow him to intimidate me.

'Spit it out, then,' I say. 'Whatever it is.'

'Did you honestly think.' He pushes his face closer to mine. 'That you'd get away with making vile comments about my fiancée and son on Facebook?'

CHAPTER FOURTEEN

'What?' I splutter.

'You heard.' Tom glares at me with absolute loathing. 'Writing vile stuff about me and my family. Attacking a *baby* for fuck's sake. Apart from being completely fucking horrible, why would you want to let everyone see what a nasty, jealous bitch you are?'

'I didn't,' I splutter in shock. 'I haven't even *been* on Facebook for over a year. I never post anything.' This was true until I looked at Tom's pictures on Monday, but I only *looked*.

I can see the beginnings of doubt in Tom's expression.

'And don't you know me better than that after ten years of being married?' I continue. 'Do you really think that I'm capable of doing something like that?'

'The facts don't lie,' Tom spits the words at me.

'Except that they do. Someone must have hacked my account because it wasn't me; I wouldn't do something like that. You know I wouldn't.'

Tom hesitates and we stand silently in the hallway.

'They're on your account,' he eventually says. 'How could someone else do that?'

'I don't know but it wasn't me. Look, come in and let's talk about it.' I walk through into the lounge and wait for him to follow me.

Tom stays out in the hallway and I wonder if he's going to leave without giving me a chance to explain. How am I in a situation where I have to defend myself for something that I didn't even do? I sit down on the sofa and tuck my hands underneath my legs to stop them from shaking. Just when I think that Tom's not going to give me a chance to explain, he comes in and sits down on the sofa opposite me.

'So what did these comments say?' I ask.

'Have a look for yourself,' he grunts.

I wait for him to show me his phone but he doesn't so after a moment I get up and go out to the kitchen to get my own. I unplug my phone from the charger and take it with me into the lounge. I sit back down and tap on the Facebook icon. I scroll through until I reach Tom's page and find the comments that I supposedly made. I gasp in horror; the comments are unbelievably vile and nasty; abusive doesn't even come close to describing them and I'm shocked that Facebook haven't suspended my account. I've wished death and misfortune on all of them but in particular, the baby, who I've also called ugly and deformed.

'Oh my God,' I gasp.

Tom stares at me, a grim expression on his face.

'They're horrible.' I scroll through and start to try to delete them but have to stop and take several deep breaths before my hands stop shaking enough for me to tap the screen properly. 'You have to believe that I didn't do this, Tom. I must have been hacked.' I'm about to delete the last comment but stop.

'Look,' I say, holding my screen up to his face. 'It shows here that I made this comment at three-thirty in the morning! I was fast asleep then.'

'But why?' Tom asks. 'Why would someone hack your account and do something like that? And how would they even know that we used to be married?'

Probably by looking at the old photos on my account of me and you, I think. I obviously don't say this because it makes me look a complete saddo who's pretending to the world that we're still together. I didn't intentionally leave them there but had never got around to deleting them. As soon as Tom's left I'll be deleting every single one of them, better late than never.

'God knows,' I say. 'Why does anyone do anything? These hackers just like to cause mischief and stir up trouble and upset. It must be sheer co-incidence that they hit lucky with the connection between us.'

'But you haven't posted comments to anyone else?' Tom says.

I can see that he doesn't know whether to believe me or not; he knows that I'm not the person to write these sort of things but equally, the evidence is there and how would someone know the previous connection between us?

The horrible thought that someone who knows me has done this pops into my mind. But who and why would someone do that? As far as I know I don't have any enemies.

'It wasn't me, Tom, so you need to stop speaking as if I did it. You know me and you know that I wouldn't do this. It's nothing more than a horrible coincidence.'

I can see Tom thinking about it; he knows that I never used to be the sort of person to do something like that no matter what happened between us. Would I have changed that much?

'Apart from anything else, why would I do this to myself,' I continue, when he doesn't answer. 'Because what would my friends think of me making those comments? It hardly makes me look like a good person, does it?'

It makes me look like a nasty, vicious bitch but what's even worse is that none of my so-called friends on Facebook have even contacted me about it. People that have known me for years have accepted that I said these things and haven't even texted me to ask what the hell's going on. But let's face it, who's bothered with me since I left Tom? A handful of friends contacted me when I first left him but soon stopped bothering when I became the awkward singleton among my happily married friends.

'I suppose when you put it like that,' Tom says, thoughtfully.

I delete the last comment and log out of Facebook and reset my password to such a complicated one that I'll no doubt forget it myself. Once Tom has left I'll have to compose a message on Facebook to announce that my account's been hacked and the vile comments were *not* made by me. Once I've done that I might close my account; it's not as if I ever look at it anyway and I don't think I could take the stress if someone hacked it again.

'So, do you believe me?' I ask.

'Yeah, I suppose I do. If I think about it, it's not the sort of thing you'd do at all.' He attempts a smile. 'But you can see why I was mad?'

'Of course I can,' I say, trying to keep the shakiness from my voice. 'But next time you want to come round here all guns blazing accusing me of something, maybe think about it first.'

'Yeah, sorry. You're right, you didn't deserve that. It's just that Gem was nearly hysterical when she saw them; she got a bit carried away and thought she had some stalking ex coming after her and Joseph. It shook me up seeing stuff written like that; someone wanting your baby dead hurts, you know. I suppose I went into super-protective mode.' He gives me a hint of the old Tom grin and I suddenly want to slap him; he's come round here shouting the odds about something that has nothing to do with me and somehow I'm seen as the ex with a problem. What about me – didn't I need protecting when we were together? It hurts that he was so ready to believe I'd do something like that. I swallow down my emotions and stand up; it's time for him to leave.

'So now that's cleared up I'll get you your mum's wedding ring.'

'No rush,' he says, but I've already seen the way his eyes lit up at the mention of it. He might as well have it, it's not as if I want it anymore although I could be really spiteful and sell it, because technically, it's mine. But I won't; he can take the ring and go and I'll never have to see him again. He can give it to his precious girlfriend and they can get married and celebrate with all of the people who once upon a time were my friends, too.

I go out into the hallway and head up the stairs and try to choke down the bitterness that rises in my throat. I don't even care about him anymore, I realise as I go into my bedroom, this unpleasant episode has completely killed any residual feelings that I might have had left for him.

Every cloud, I suppose.

I open the top drawer of my dressing table and take out the envelope containing my Decree Absolute. I open the envelope flap and put my fingers in and pull out my ex-mother-in-law's engagement ring. I turn it around and study it and the old-fashioned cut diamond catches the light; it's a very nice ring and most likely worth a decent amount of money. Perhaps I should have sold it. I wonder how Gem-the-secretary will feel about wearing the ex-wife's engagement ring? It might be a family heirloom but I don't think I would like it if there'd been a wife before me and I hope she doesn't either. I hope she secretly hates it and thinks that Tom is a cheap-skate for giving it to her.

I'm about to close the envelope flap and return it to the drawer when I feel that there's something else inside apart from the Decree Absolute. I turn the envelope upside down and give it a little shake.

I stand and watch in shock as my locket falls out of the envelope and onto the dressing table.

CHAPTER
FIFTEEN

'All done then, love, here's your keys,' the locksmith says, handing me three sets of shiny new keys.

'Thank you.'

'Three for each door,' he says, as he packs away his tools. 'Just in case you lose one.'

I laugh at his unfunny joke. I told him that I'd lost a whole set of my house keys to explain the fact that I wanted both the front door and the back door locks replaced. I said that I didn't know who might have picked them up and I couldn't take the risk of someone being able to get into my house.

He explained that I might to be able to claim for the cost of replacement locks – two hundred and fifty-pounds – on my house insurance, as lost keys are covered on most policies. He said I'd probably need to ring the police and report it to do that. He said I might be lucky because there was always the possibility that someone might have handed them in. I nodded and said that I'd look into it but of course I won't, because I haven't lost my keys at all.

He liked to chat and also said something else very interesting; he gets called to lots of houses that people have just moved into to replace the locks. Apparently, a lot of people who move into a new home get all of the locks replaced immediately as they have no idea how many sets of keys are floating around estate agents, ex-owners and any number of random people. Realistically, there could be no end of people with keys to a house that you've just bought and you would have no way of knowing. I never considered this when I bought this house, the thought never entered my head.

But it has now.

Because I'm sure that someone has been in my house and I'm convinced that Diana is that person.

After Tom left yesterday – I gave him the engagement ring and he couldn't get away fast enough – I sat down and composed a suitably gushing Facebook post to explain that my account had been hacked. I said that the vile comments on my profile weren't made by me and that I didn't agree with them in any way. Sickeningly, I felt obliged to wish Tom, Gem and the baby well and state that there was no ill feeling between us. I also deleted all the photos of Tom that were on my profile. Once I'd got that out of the way I sat down and tried to understand how my silver locket could possibly be in the envelope with my Decree Absolute.

No matter what scenario I imagined, I couldn't see any way on earth that I would have put it there myself and then forgotten that I'd done so. I turned this house upside down looking for it, admittedly I didn't look in the envelope but I had no need to; that envelope has been in that drawer since I moved in and I have definitely not looked at or removed it since I've been here. There has been no reason to. There is no way possible or any reason why I would have put my locket in that envelope.

Which leaves only one possibility.

Someone else put it there.

I am certain that someone is Diana.

My theory is that she has a key to this house because the previous owner, Jayne, gave her one; maybe to water the plants or something, or maybe Diana just talked her into it like she's tried to talk me into doing her tax return. I think she came in when I was at work yesterday and put the locket that she found in the street in the drawer.

Or maybe she never found it in the street at all; maybe she came in here and took it. I'm almost sure that she also made the comments on my Facebook account because it's too much of a coincidence for it not to be her. I would have no idea how to hack someone else's Facebook account because it's not something that I would want to do but who's to say that it's not easy? Like everything else, I've no doubt that you can do an internet search for instructions on how to do it. I have no idea what Diana is capable of and if she can lie to my face, sticking a few comments on Facebook isn't a huge leap. She could log in anywhere as me and I would have no clue.

Yes, it does seem far-fetched and unlikely that my next door neighbour would do something like this but there is no other possible explanation for what's happened.

Apart from one.

And that is that I put the locket in the drawer myself and also that I posted the vile comments on Facebook. For this to have happened I would have had to somehow do all of this without knowing that I was doing it; that somehow, I'm suffering from some sort of amnesia. This possibility is even more far-fetched than Diana coming into my house so I've discounted it; I am not mad.

It was Diana.

The sensible part of me knows that this is also an insane idea. Is Diana so twisted that she has done these things because I've given her the cold shoulder? I cannot think of any other explanation yet rationally, I know that it sounds quite mad. Who would behave in such a way just because I spurned their friendship? It's not normal behaviour but she's obviously not normal.

So although it's cost me money, having the locks changed will prove my theory either way; if my locket disappears again, then clearly it won't be Diana doing it as she won't be able to get in to my house. As to my Facebook account, I've changed the password and also changed my settings so that if anyone tries to log on elsewhere I'll get an email. Even so; I will be checking my account every morning to make sure that nothing else appears on there.

'Cash or card, love?' The locksmith is looking at me expectantly and I realise that I've drifted off again.

'Sorry.' I reach into my back pocket and give him two hundred and fifty pounds in cash that I drew out from the cash point this morning.

'Cheers.' He tucks it carefully into a battered, black zip-up pouch which he pushes into his toolbox before closing the lid. He picks up the old locks from the front and back door from the floor and offers them to me.

I look at him blankly.

'Don't you want them? They might come in handy for a shed or something. You've still got other keys for them.'

'Oh, thanks.' I take them from him. There's only one place they'll be going and that's in the bin.

'Cheers, love, have a good one.' He picks up his toolbox and stomps off down the path to his van which has *ABC Locksmiths* emblazoned on the side. I smile to myself as I shut the front door behind him.

I hope Diana notices the van.

If she does, she'll know that I know what she's been up to and she'll also know that she won't be getting into my house ever again

* * *

'You think your next door neighbour has been coming in your house when you're not there?' I can't see Ben's face because we're speaking on the phone but I can hear something in his voice that I don't like. He rang just after the locksmith left to tell me that he's going to put his flat on the market and move back home. I was delighted to hear this, and even though I know that one of the reasons is his split from Monica, he sounded upbeat and excited about the future so I think he's getting over her. I then told him all about Tom's visit yesterday and how I'd found my locket and who I think has been doing it.

'Yes,' I say. 'I do. There's no other explanation for what's happened but she won't be doing it again because I've had the locks changed.

'But why?' Ben asks. 'I mean, why would she do that? You hardly know her, do you? You've only spoken to her a few times.'

'God knows, she's obviously not right in the head,' I say. 'But now she won't be able to get in here so nothing else will happen and that will prove that it's her.'

There's silence and I open my mouth to speak and then close it again. I know that Ben is thinking it over and I don't want to start gabbling and over-explaining myself because it'll just sound as if I'm trying to justify myself. I wish now that I hadn't told him about it because when I say it out loud it does sound quite mad. There was no reason for him to know about any of it now that I come to think about it; me and my big mouth.

'So. Let me get this straight,' Ben says, slowly. 'You couldn't find your locket and you think you saw her wearing it. You asked her; she said she hasn't got a locket. You then found the locket in your bedroom and decided that she's been in your house when you're not there and put it in your room. She's also been making vile comments to Tom on your Facebook account and she's been doing all this because you refused to have coffee with her?'

I sigh. I really wish I hadn't told him now because put like that it does sound as if I'm slightly unhinged.

'Well when you say it like that, it sounds ridiculous but believe me, I'm not going mad. She's been in here, I can feel it. She's been playing weird music really loudly in the early hours of the morning as well. Strange laughing and singing and stuff.' I know I'm exaggerating, it only happened once but I want Ben to know how I feel. It may sound insane when I say it out loud but I know that Diana's doing it.

I just know.

'Loud music? That's not really weird, though, is it?' Ben says. 'The flat next door to me plays loud music all day and all night but I don't think he's out to get me, he's just a thoughtless, selfish tosser. Even if she is round the bend, how would she know that you and Tom were married? It's not likely, is it, sis? And how could she get onto your Facebook? And there's no way she could know that you were going to look in that envelope and find your locket.'

She couldn't have known I was going to look there – I didn't even know it myself. The doubts start to creep in but I shake them away; *I'm* not the mad one.

'Who knows but time will tell,' I say airily, keen to change the subject or get him off the phone. 'And the weird things will stop happening now which will prove that I'm right. I'm going to start checking my Facebook account every day, too. And she could easily have seen the old photos of Tom on my account and put two and two together. I've deleted them now, anyway, I should have done it ages ago.'

'It's a bit of a stretch, though, isn't it? Why would she bother? And what if the weird things don't stop?' asks Ben.

'Then I'm the one who's going mad.' I laugh.

'I'm being serious.'

'I don't know what you mean,' I say, although I think I do. 'What do you mean?'

'Nothing,' Ben says, quietly. 'Forget it.'

'I don't want to forget it,' I say, a bit too loudly. 'I want you to tell me what you mean.'

Ben sighs.

'Well?' I demand.

'Okay, I'm just going to say it even though you're not going to like it.'

'Just spit it out,' I snap.

'Okay, okay. All I'm saying is that it wouldn't be the first time something like this has happened, would it? Because you've done stuff before without realising you've done it.'

There's a horrible silence after he's spoken and I think we both know that a line has been crossed.

'Frida?'

'How can you even say something like that?' I say, swallowing down the lump in my throat. 'I thought you were supposed to be on my side. I thought you had my back.'

'Of course I've got your back, you know I have. I'm only saying this because I care about you. Be honest Frida, why would a neighbour you barely know break into your house and do things like that?'

'She didn't break in, she has a key,' I say.

'You're not being rational about it,' Ben sighs. 'I'm worried about you, I don't want you getting ill again.'

'I'm fine.' I say.

'But are you?' Ben asks quietly. 'Because you said you were fine before but you weren't.'

I shrug and then remember that Ben can't see me.

'Frida?'

'I'm here.'

'Have you told Mum?' he asks.

'You must be joking, why on earth would I tell her about it? She'd go into mother hen mode and insist that I go and stay with her.'

'Might not be a bad idea,' Ben says, quietly.

'Don't you dare tell her, Ben. If you do I'll never speak to you again.'

'Don't shut me out, Frida,' Ben says. 'Last time you promised me that you'd never shut me out again.'

'I don't know what you're talking about.'

'Yes you do,' Ben suddenly shouts, making me jump. 'You had a fucking breakdown and you wouldn't even talk about it and now you're doing exactly the same thing again.'

I don't answer but take the phone away from my ear and press the *end call* button.

CHAPTER SIXTEEN

Monday morning dawns and I feel like death.

When the screech of the alarm clock finally penetrates my consciousness I drag myself out of bed and stumble to the bathroom as if I were eighty years old. Somehow I manage to haul myself into the shower and I turn the water on as hot as I can bear it and stand underneath it hoping to feel better. As I lather my hair up with shampoo I reflect on the weekend – a completely wasted weekend as it transpired. After I hung up on Ben he called me back over and over again but I refused to answer. I sent him a text saying that I was fine but I didn't want to talk about it anymore as I couldn't see the point. He replied immediately saying that he was going to tell Mum about me and that he'd come and stay with me as soon as he'd finished the job he was working on. The way he said it, it didn't sound like I had a choice about him coming to stay and I felt furious with myself for opening my big mouth to him. There's no way I want Mum knowing; she'll just start fretting and worrying and driving me mad with constantly checking up on me. So I texted him back and told him that I was going to make a doctor's appointment as soon as they open this morning. I promised him that I was going to get help this time and not shut him out but warned him that if he told Mum, I was never going to speak to him again. Good old blackmail, in other words. After dozens more texts he finally agreed not to tell her but only if I promised to ring him after my appointment and let him know how I got on.

I *am* fine. Yes, I did have a breakdown of sorts after Tom and I split up but it wasn't as bad as Ben makes out – I just needed to work through things in my own way and in my own time.

We don't all have to talk everything to death.

Okay, apparently I *did* send some strange text messages to Tom but I really don't remember. It was the pills that made me do it; I foolishly accepted a prescription from the doctor but they made me so fuzzy headed that I couldn't seem to think straight. Once I stopped taking them I started to feel a lot better and just got on with things. If Tom hadn't been so gutless he'd have spoken to me directly instead of panicking Ben by contacting him and telling him that I was suicidal just because I'd sent him a few texts. And actually, I think I was allowed to go a bit off the scale; I'd just found out my husband had been cheating and lying to me for ten years and I think anyone would have struggled with that.

Even if I do speak to a doctor, what am I supposed to say? I know that a visit will only result in more pills because that's all there is to offer; unless they have me committed of course, but that's unlikely as the mental health units are already all full to bursting so they won't have any room for me. I'm sure that this time is different; it's Diana who's the problem, not me.

Nevertheless, after the texting marathon with Ben I couldn't settle and spent the rest of Saturday and the whole of Sunday aimlessly drifting around the house and questioning myself; asking myself if I really am *fine*.

I eventually concluded that I am despite the fact that I haven't slept well this last week and am not feeling great. When I wake in the morning I feel exhausted and as if I've been working hard all night, not resting. It's not that I'm not sleeping; I am, but I wake up feeling more tired than when I went to bed. This is of course due to the Diana situation. Now that she can no longer get into my house I should be feeling better – the fact that I'm not is because I now have to prove my sanity to Ben. I've questioned myself repeatedly – could I have hidden my locket and not remembered? Could it have been me who made the comments on

Facebook? Because it's true that I *did* look at Tom's account.

But I honestly felt no anger or hatred when I viewed his posts and if I felt nothing then why would I make such vile comments? And the locket – why would I do something like that, it just makes no sense.

I am most definitely not the person that I was a year ago but I need to prove this to Ben because if I can't, he's going to tell Mum and then I'll have both of them worrying about me.

To prove to myself that I'm not going mad I'm going to find out if Diana definitely had a key and if she didn't then maybe I *will* make a doctor's appointment. Maybe. The only way to find this out is to ask the previous owner of this house if she gave Diana a key.

So I've decided. I'm going into town after work today and I'm going to the jewellers shop to ask Jayne.

* * *

I put on a brave face at the mini market but Phoebe has still asked me several times if I'm okay so I guess I'm not as good an actress as I think I am. The third time she asked I told her that I had a headache and this resulted in her insisting that I go home and have a lie down. I told her I was fine and maybe I snapped a little bit because she didn't ask me again. I felt like a proper low-life then and thought that maybe I shouldn't have gone to work in the first place. I don't know why I did; I've always been the same – I'd go into work even if I was dying and had to drag myself there. When I left Tom I only took one day off work and that was the day I moved out of our house. I lied and told my manager that I had a migraine and went back into work the following day as if nothing had happened and I never told any of my work colleagues that Tom and I had split up until months later. I should definitely have taken some time off then; I wasn't really up to concentrating on a demanding job and when I left it wasn't only because I wanted a change, it was because I'd lost my confidence.

Maybe I could learn something from this.

As soon as my shift ends I bid goodbye to Phoebe and walk home as quickly as possible to pick my car up. I don't bother wasting time having lunch but get straight into my car and zoom off into town. I want to get this over and done with so that I can pacify Ben and get my life back to normal. It's only as I'm parking in the multi-storey car park that I realise that I do actually have a headache which is probably due to the fact that I didn't eat any breakfast. Also, the only drink that I've had today is the coffee that Phoebe bought out to me at ten o'clock so I'm probably dehydrated as well. I'll have to have something to eat when I get home and then maybe I'll feel better. This visit to Jayne shouldn't take very long – I just need to know that Diana has, or rather *had*, a key to my house and then I can rest assured that I'm not going mad and that it's her that's been doing these things.

I park the car and hurry to the ticket machine and rummage in my bag for change. I can only find enough coins for one hour but surely that will be enough – how long does it take to ask one question? I just hope that Jayne is working today; I need to know now because I don't think I can wait another day to find out. Although if she's not working I'll have no choice because the shop owner is hardly likely to hand over her address to a perfect stranger.

I march quickly through town to the jewellers on Jubilee Street and with a rattle of the old-fashioned bell announcing my arrival, I enter the shop. I'm relieved to see Jayne standing behind the counter and smile with relief. She doesn't smile back and doesn't look particularly pleased to see me – in fact she looks quite the opposite.

'Hello, Jayne,' I say, breezily, as if we're old friends. 'How are you?'

She purses her lips and looks over her shoulder to check that the owner is not in earshot.

'What do you want?'

I'm surprised at her bluntness but I try to hide it behind a fake smile.

'Just a question about your old next door neighbour,' I say.

She stares at me, unsmilingly, before speaking.

'I've nothing to say. Unless you want to buy something I'm afraid I can't help you.'

'It's just one simple question – a yes or no,' I say.

'I'll get Mr Plummer to help you if you want to buy something,' she says, ignoring my question. She turns away to walk into the back of the shop and I see my chance of finding out about the key disappearing.

'Please,' I say. 'It's just one question.'

'No. You need to leave. Now.'

I stare at her and realise that she doesn't want to talk to me and I'm going to have to speak to a doctor and somehow prove that I'm not going insane or having a nervous breakdown. I feel suddenly exhausted with it all and my head is pounding and I feel sick. I've already turned to leave when her parting words to me the last time we met pop into my head.

Don't tell anyone that you saw me.

'Okay, I'll go,' I say, turning back to face her, knowing that what I'm about to say will sound completely ridiculous. 'But when I get home I'm going to tell the whole street that I saw you today.'

Her mouth drops open and she gawps at me.

'And,' I add. 'I'll tell them you never went to Australia at all.'

CHAPTER
SEVENTEEN

I bite into the toasted teacake and slowly chew it. It's dry and, I suspect, stale, and the miniscule scraping of butter on it isn't improving it. Nevertheless I chomp it around my mouth and eventually manage to swallow it by washing it down with a swig of tea.

Jayne has promised to join me here at one o'clock when she has her lunch break. It's now five to one. When I made my silly threat about telling the whole street that she hadn't gone to Australia, her face visibly paled and for a moment I felt awful that I'd said it. She then whispered that she would meet me here and that she would *explain everything*. I was about to tell her that I only had one question which she could quickly answer yes or no to and then I'd be on my way, but then I thought that I should really apologise to her. The very least

I can do is to buy her a cup of tea and a sandwich for pitching up at her workplace and demanding that she talk to me. I'm also going to reassure her that I would *never* tell anyone in the street that she hasn't really gone to Australia. She's obviously still completely mortified and isn't able to cope with the embarrassment.

Although I won't tell her that until she's answered my question about the key.

I check my watch for what feels like the twentieth time to see that it's gone one o'clock. I'm just starting to think that Jayne isn't coming when the café door opens and she comes in. I put my hand up in a wave to get her attention as the only free table was right at the back and I'm out of sight of the door. I don't want her to think that I'm not here. She spots me and makes her way over, nodding to the man behind the counter on the way.

'Can I get you a drink?' I offer as she slides into the seat opposite. 'And a sandwich? Or a toasted teacake?'

'No, I'm fine, thank you. Joe will bring me my usual.'

On cue, the man from behind the counter, who I assume is Joe, appears at the table and places a cheese sandwich and a coffee in front of her. She thanks him and he bustles back behind the counter.

'You have some questions?' She picks up her sandwich and takes a delicate bite and then replaces it on the plate.

'Just one, really,' I say, feeling rather foolish.

She raises an eyebrow and I realise she's not going to make it easy for me and I can't say that I blame her.

'Okay,' I say. 'I just need to know if you gave the next door neighbour a key to your, my, house. Diana, that is, not Bert. That's all. Just one simple question.'

'I did not.'

'Oh, okay.' I feel immediately deflated but then remind myself that she only lived in the house for a short time – the owner before Jayne must have given Diana a key. Which kind of makes sense, thinking about it, because Jayne would hardly build a seven foot high fence for privacy from her next door neighbour and then give her a key to her house.

'Is that it?' Jayne asks. 'Is that all you wanted to know?'

'Um, I think so. You didn't live in the house for very long, did you?'

'No.'

'So I suppose the owner before you could have given Diana a key.'

'Possibly,' she says, taking another bite from her sandwich. 'Why do you ask?'

I look at Jayne and try to read the look on her face; if I tell her the truth she's going to think, like Ben, that I'm deranged.

'I think my neighbour has a key and she's been in my house,' I blurt out, deciding that I'll never have to see her again so who cares if she thinks I'm mad.

Jayne pauses mid bite and carefully lowers her sandwich onto the plate. She stares down at it without speaking before looking up at me.

'She can't have,' she says.

'I know it sounds mad but...' I begin.

'No.' She shakes her head. 'I mean she can't have a key. I had all of the locks changed.'

So Diana hasn't been in the house at all and I'm the one that's mad. I look at Jayne and I realise what the expression is on her face.

It's pity.

I feel suddenly choked and I fight back the tears that threaten to engulf me. I really believed that I was better and on an even keel, I thought my life was on track again but it's so not; I've been fooling myself.

I must have hidden the locket.

I must have posted the Facebook messages.

I've done these things and I have no recollection of them at all, nothing, not even the vaguest memory. A feeling of panic threatens to overwhelm me and I feel fear, real fear, at what else I might be capable of doing without even knowing.

I reach underneath the table and grab hold of my handbag and stand up.

'I'm so sorry that I barged into the shop like that, Jayne,' I say. 'And just so you know, I would never, ever, tell anyone in the street that you're not in Australia. I don't even know why I said it. Thank you for your help and I'm so sorry to have bothered you.'

I just need to get out of here and think.

I need to talk to Ben.

I need to make a doctor's appointment

'Don't go,' Jayne says, quietly.

I look down at her.

'Sorry?'

'Sit down.'

I look at her in confusion.

'Please,' she says. 'Sit down. There are things you need to know.'

* * *

'First of all, I'm sorry.' Jayne picks her sandwich up and then puts it back down on the plate again before pushing the whole thing into the middle of the table.

'For what?' I ask.

'For selling you the house. I was really hoping that a man would buy it. Maybe it would have been different if I'd sold it to a man. But I was desperate, you see, and no one else made an offer so I had no choice but to take yours.'

'I have no idea what you're talking about.'

'And to be fair,' Jayne continues, as if I haven't spoken. 'I thought it was just me. I didn't *know* that she would do the same thing again, although I suspected. So I'm sorry about that and if I could help in any way, I would, but I can't.'

She looks at me as if this will mean something

and when I say nothing she sighs heavily.

'Okay. So what you need to do is very simple. It's not ideal and I know you only moved in a matter of weeks ago but there's nothing else for it; you'll have to sell up and move out and hope that once you're gone she'll leave you alone. Hopefully, out of her sight, will be out of her mind.'

Unable to help myself, I burst out laughing.

'I'm sorry to laugh, but I have no intention of moving,' I say. 'I love the house. Why would I want to leave?'

Jayne smiles sadly.

'You remind me so much of myself,' she says, quietly.

I try hard not to feel insulted; in no way, shape or form are we anything like each other.

'I wasn't always like this you know,' she says, as if she can read my thoughts. 'I was just like you once; optimistic and happy, full of life. I had a good job and a great group of friends and I never thought that one person could ruin my life, but she did. When I bought that house I thought that I had it all and I couldn't believe how lucky I was. Now I'm on my own and hiding away in case she finds me. I really did want to move to Australia but I just didn't have the guts after everything that happened. I've lost everything because of her and you will too if you stay there. It doesn't matter that you've changed the locks, I did that and it didn't stop her. She's doesn't need to get in to destroy you.'

'You mean Diana?' I say.

'Yes. Diana. The witch. She'll do it to you because it's already started. She's clever; at the beginning I wasn't even sure if it was her or if I was letting my imagination run away with me. Take my advice and leave now while you still have your life. Don't go back there, stay with a relative or a friend and put the house on the market. Try and sell it to a man; maybe she won't get away with it then.'

'I think you're being ridiculous,' I say, unable to help myself. 'I agree that Diana is odd and I'm sure that she's been in my house somehow even though you say you never gave her a key, but she's certainly not dangerous and she doesn't frighten me. She's just a rather sad, nasty woman trying to cause mischief because she has no life of her own.'

Jayne shakes her head.

'You're so wrong. How do you think she got a key? She would have *made* the estate agent give it to her. She *makes* people do things and if they don't do what she wants then she ruins their lives. That was my mistake – I underestimated her. I thought I could put a big fence up and ignore her but I couldn't.'

I feel immense relief that I'm not going mad; Diana could easily have obtained a key from the estate agents. Knowing how pushy and over-bearing she is I've no doubt that the very young estate agent who showed me around would have handed a key to her if she'd demanded it. He didn't seem overly concerned with security – when I visited the agency office I witnessed him give a key to a prospective buyer of an empty house rather than bother to show him around himself.

'Why do you think Diana wanted to destroy you?' I ask gently. 'Did you argue with her or fall out over something?'

Jayne laughs; she sounds on the verge of hysteria and I see Joe look over at us from behind the counter.

'She doesn't need a reason; she does it because she *can*. She enjoys it. She's insane. I was friendly to her at first but then I started to avoid her because I couldn't breathe without her being there in my face the whole time. She was forever banging on my front door for one reason or another and I felt that she wanted to take over my life. The reason I had the fence put up was to stop her appearing at my back door uninvited. I think that's what made her turn on me.'

She gazes down at her fingers; the skin is red raw around her nails and she begins to pick at the skin and tear it and I have to look away. I feel very sorry for her; Jayne is obviously not a well person to have let Diana get to her so much.

'She's clever and devious and she'll never do anything in front of witnesses but believe me, she'll ruin your life. I lost my job because of her and all of my friends deserted me and it's all her fault,' Jayne's voice is getting louder and shriller. 'You'll wish you'd listened to me if you go back there. Please don't go back.'

'Look, it's okay, Jayne. I'm fine.' I take her hand and pull it away from her fingers and try to reassure her. 'Nothing's going to happen to me. If by the remotest chance I start to feel threatened at all I'll be straight down to the nearest police station so there's really no need to worry.'

I feel awful; Jayne has some serious issues and Diana seems to feature heavily in them and by asking her about the key I've stirred them all up. I should have realised the state she was in by the way she reacted to my threat to tell everyone she hadn't gone to Australia. It wasn't a rational reaction and I feel ashamed that I've done this to her.

Jayne pulls her hand away from me and stands up.

'I have to go or else I'll be late for work. Please promise me that you won't go back to that house.'

'Honestly, Jayne,' I say. 'There's no need to worry, I'll be fine.'

She pulls the strap of her handbag over her shoulder and grips it tightly.

'I know you don't believe me and you think I'm exaggerating but I'm not,' she says. 'You need to sell the house before it's too late.'

I have no idea what to say, so I stay silent.

'She won't stop, you know,' she says. 'You'll have to kill her to make her stop.'

I look at her in shock, unable to believe what I'm hearing.

Jayne leans down and across the table towards me.

'That's what she told me,' she whispers. 'She said if I wanted my life back, I'd have to kill her first.'

She smiles and I sit mute, unable to think of anything to say.

'I wish I had,' she laughs her shrill laugh again and I wonder what I've done to this woman by dredging up the past.

'Jayne, I...' I begin to say.

'So, there's your choice,' she says, straightening up and smiling an almost manic smile.

'Leave the house or kill her.'

CHAPTER EIGHTEEN

After Jayne's gone I sit for a while and try to make sense of what she's told me. She's obviously terrified of Diana and thinks that she's out to get her. I think that Jayne is definitely not a well person and it sounds as if Diana did the same to her as she's done to me and Jayne is blaming her for her life falling apart. I think that Diana probably caused a bit of trouble to Jayne, like she has to me, but as to ruining Jayne's life? I don't think that's possible.

Diana doesn't frighten me but I can see that she could easily be intimidating to someone like Jayne. Her assertion that Diana is mad might be stretching it a bit but what sort of person lets themselves into their neighbour's house and takes something and wears it and then puts it back? Because the more I think about it the more convinced I am that she took the locket from my house. Would a normal person hack their neighbour's Facebook account and let themselves into their home?

Of course they don't.

Who knows what else she could have done once she was in my home; my laptop is sitting on the shelf underneath the coffee table so she could easily have looked at that. Thankfully, it has nothing on it except my browsing history. Tom and I used to share a laptop and when I left him I never took it with me but simply deleted everything on it that was mine. I eventually bought myself a new one but rarely use it except for looking at stuff to buy. Even so, as soon as I get home I'm going to change all of my passwords on every single online account that I can think of. I don't think there's any way she could do anything without my mobile phone but I'm not taking any chances.

I'm not afraid of Diana but I should certainly be wary of her; if she can come into my house without my permission, who knows what else she could do if she's given the opportunity. Thank God I've had the locks changed. It does creep me out to think that she's been in my house when I'm not there and I have to keep reminding myself that she has done this and that I'm *not* imagining it because it just seems so unbelievable. Part of me feels that I should just confront her and have it out with her and get it into the open because actually, *how dare she*.

Then I remember how she totally blanked me

over the locket; she point blank lied to my face and had no problem in doing so. Realistically, if I go storming round to see her, she's not going to admit anything so all I'll have done is inflame the situation. Now that I've had the locks changed she won't be able to get in and do anything else.

I could and *should* go to the police; the very fact that she's been in my house without my permission is surely an offence. She may have had a key to my house but I never gave it to her and she had absolutely no right to enter my property. I should make a complaint because why should she get away with it? People like her need to be taught that they can't go around doing whatever they want as if they're above the law.

But I can't.

I have no proof that's she been in my house; not one shred of evidence. My own brother is all too ready to believe that I'm going round the bend so the police are highly unlikely to believe me and they're hardly going to make it a top priority investigation. I could ask them to speak to Jayne to confirm what Diana is like but do I really want to put her through that? That's if Jayne would even talk to the police; I have a suspicion that she wouldn't.

I look around the cafe to see that the lunchtime rush has finished and I'm the only person left in here, lingering over a cold cup of tea. Joe is leaning against the counter reading a newspaper and I feel guilty that I've spent over an hour in here and have spent the sum total of two-pounds-fifty on the lunchtime special of a tea cake and a cup of tea. I rummage around in my handbag and shove a pound coin underneath the saucer to make myself feel better. I glance at my watch and realise that I've overstayed on my parking ticket; my procrastinating over Diana and Jayne has probably resulted in a fine.

Great; the perfect end to a perfect morning.

Not.

* * *

I didn't get a parking ticket; luckily for me it must be a slow day for the traffic wardens and I'm still congratulating myself when I pull up outside my house. I'm surprised to see that Diana is leaning against the garden wall talking to Bert. She's normally at work on Mondays so today must be a day off. Despite my assertion of not being afraid of her I feel my heart start to pound at the sight of her and as I get out of the car, instead of heading towards my house I find that my feet are carrying me towards her and Bert. The heart pounding is not fear, I tell myself, but my reaction to confrontation.

Because despite my assertion that I was going to ignore her, I realise that I can't. I'm going to confront her and demand to know why she thinks she can come into my house as she pleases.

'Good afternoon,' Diana turns to greet me with a wide grin. 'We were just talking about you.'

'Really?' I demand. 'And what were you saying?'

'I was just telling Bert that I saw a locksmith's van outside your house and we were wondering why. Weren't we, Bert?'

I study her face; her smile looks triumphant and I'm sure that she's taunting me; daring me to question her.

'Can't you guess why?' I ask.

'Well,' Diana says. 'I did wonder if you might have had a break in. Have the police been round? I thought they might have visited us and asked us if we'd noticed anything suspicious, wouldn't you Bert?'

I look at Bert, who looks sheepish and won't meet my eye.

'You know very well why I've had the locks changed, Diana,' I say evenly.

'Me?' Diana's eyes widen and she looks at me and then Bert. 'Why would I know why you've had the locks changed? How could *I* possibly know?'

I stare at her and she doesn't flinch or even look slightly uncomfortable. As I expected she's just going to deny it and there's nothing I can do about that but I'm going to have my say anyway; I want her to know that I know what she's done. I'm not Jayne and she's not going to intimidate me into moving away; she needs to know that she's met her match.

'I *have* been broken into, only the person who did it had a key and let themselves in so they didn't need to actually break in.' I stare at her.

'I'm sorry, you've lost me.' Diana affects a puzzled look.

'The person who broke in was *you*. You have a key to my house and have let yourself in, probably on many occasions. I've had the locks changed to make sure that you can never do it again.' There, I've said it now and it's all out in the open.

'I beg your pardon?' she asks.

'You heard,' I say bluntly. 'You've been going in my house when I'm not there but now you won't be able to.'

Diana bursts out laughing.

'And why on earth would I do that? Tell me, what did I steal?'

I stare at her and realise that it's pointless to even talk about it to her so I say nothing.

'You.' Diana points her finger at me. 'Are talking absolute rubbish so I'm going to give you the benefit of the doubt and assume that you're joking, because if you're not,' she moves closer and stares down at me. 'I'm going to have to make a complaint about you destroying my good character.'

I stop myself from stepping backwards, determined to hold my ground.

'I'm not destroying your character, I'm telling you that I know what you've been doing and that I've put a stop to it. I haven't said it to anyone else but I want you to know.' I'm about to tell her that I've spoken to Jayne but manage to stop myself; if I say anything about Jayne then Diana will guess that she hasn't left town.

Diana's smile grows wider.

'Well, you've said it in front of Bert, which strictly speaking is defamation of character but I'll let it go on this occasion because I think you might be imagining things, my dear. Maybe you've been overdoing it. Perhaps,' she smirks. 'You need to see a doctor.'

'I'm not the one who needs to see a doctor,' I snap. 'And I'm not *your dear*. There's nothing wrong with *me* but going into someone else's house without their permission is hardly normal behaviour, is it? Maybe you're the one who needs to see a doctor.'

She thrusts her face inches from mine.

'Well if you're so sure I've been in your house, Miss Sherlock, why don't you just go ahead and prove it,' she says, quietly.

'So you're admitting it?' I ask.

'I'm not admitting anything. You're unhinged. Why on earth would I want to break into your house?'

I glance towards Bert who has been watching us intently; he must have heard what I've said to Diana.

'What are you looking at Bert for?' Diana laughs, following my gaze. 'Perhaps you should take Bert with you when you make your preposterous accusation to the police. Or have you already told them? Oh, of course you haven't,' she says, noting my silence. 'Because you'd need evidence for that, wouldn't you?'

'What do you think, Bert?' I ask, ignoring her. 'Do you think it's okay to enter someone's house without their permission?'

Diana turns to stare at Bert. 'Do tell, Bert, what do you think of your next door neighbour's wild accusations?'

Bert shuffles awkwardly and I feel sad that I've put him in this situation. I'm already regretting confronting Diana; it was pointless and has achieved nothing. Although on the plus side she's never likely to ask me in for a coffee again.

Bert stays silent and meets my eyes for the briefest of moments before dropping his gaze to his feet. His expression reminds me of Jayne's face earlier today when I threatened to tell the street that she hadn't gone to Australia.

He looks absolutely terrified.

CHAPTER NINETEEN

I lie in bed and open my eyes and try to think what day it is.

Tuesday, it's Tuesday.

Over a week since my confrontation with Diana. I should be feeling good because since I accused her I've heard nothing; no more Facebook comments or disappearing lockets because she can no longer get in. I haven't seen her at all and she hasn't been knocking on my door demanding that I do her tax return, either. Although I hadn't intended confronting her it's had the desired effect of making her leave me alone. Life has returned to being peaceful and uneventful.

I should be feeling good, but somehow, I'm not. It's all over now, I keep reassuring myself, but somehow I don't feel the relief that I should be feeling.

This is no doubt due to the fact that I haven't been sleeping well; I thought that my sleep would improve now that my house is secure but it hasn't. Each night I fall into a deep, heavy sleep and dream bizarre dreams that in the first seconds of waking seem very real. In those first few seconds I remember the dream vividly but as soon as I try to think about it and make sense of it, it sputters away before I can grab hold of it. I'm sure that my dreams are trying to tell me something important.

I can feel it.

Or maybe I'm imagining things and trying to find something to worry about because I didn't think that getting rid of Diana would be so easy; I expected to have a fight on my hands. She's been ominously quiet and there has been no repeat of the music playing in the small hours. If I'm honest, after Jayne told me what she did to her I'm surprised that she's backed off so easily. I'm hoping that it's because she's realised that I'm nothing like Jayne and she can't bully me.

I haven't told anyone about my confrontation with Diana; not Ben, not Mum, not Phoebe. When I left Diana and Bert and came into the house, the first thing I did was to pull my mobile out of my bag to ring Ben to update him on what had happened. I wanted to tell him about Jayne so that he'd realise that I'm not imagining things; that Diana has history for doing weird things and that I'm not overreacting.

But I thought about it for a while and then put

my mobile away again. I did ring him later that evening when I felt calmer but I never mentioned Diana; I lied and told him that I'd been for an appointment with my doctor. I said that he'd put me forward for counselling and I was waiting for an appointment. I said that I felt better for having talked about it and thanked him for making me realise that I needed help. I could hear the relief in Ben's voice and I felt disgust with myself; I've never lied to my brother before.

Should I have told him the truth? I'm not sure.

Because I've started to doubt myself; the whole thing seems so far-fetched and unbelievable. Why? Why would Diana have done these things? What would she achieve?

Absolutely nothing.

I've tried to convince myself that I haven't let my imagination run riot, because of what Jayne has told me about Diana but I have to be honest; I don't think that Jayne is a stable person.

Maybe I'm not a stable person.

Was the look of fear on Bert's face because of me? Is it me that he's afraid of? I can't help thinking this because I haven't seen Bert since my confrontation with Diana; his door has been firmly closed and I don't feel I can call on him in case his reaction confirms that it's me that he's afraid of.

Because he could be thinking that *I'm* the deranged one and not Diana.

I saw the same look on Jayne's face – am I misreading the situation? Am I the threatening one and not Diana? I don't like this rabbit hole that my mind is going down but I can't ignore these thoughts because I know from experience that doing that never ends well. I have to confront my issues and ask myself difficult questions about my own mental health because I didn't cope very well when Tom and I split up. I can fool myself that I left my job because I wanted a change but deep down I know that the real reason is that I couldn't do it anymore. I struggled to get through a day at work because all I wanted to do was cry and howl at how unfair life was but I wouldn't allow myself to do that in front of anyone. I should have taken time off but being the stubborn idiot that I am, I was determined to soldier on as if nothing had happened.

God knows why.

Maybe it was pride; I've never been one to show my feelings so perhaps it was. I thought that the anti-depressants could somehow fix a broken heart. They couldn't, of course, only time can do that. Once I started taking the tablets I spent the days drifting around like a ghost, unable to concentrate or hold any sort of meaningful conversation. They might work for other people but they didn't for me because I wasn't depressed, I was sad. So I gave my notice in for a job that meant everything to me and had taken me years to work my way up to rather than admit that I couldn't cope. I didn't even work my notice but took holiday so that I could leave immediately. I think it was a relief for everyone as my missed deadlines and vacant expression were becoming embarrassing and it says something about how bad things were that they let me go so quickly. Against Mum's wishes I then decided that I needed to move out of her spare room and into a place of my own. I wanted to be independent and not have Mum's concerned face confronting me at every turn. I theorised that if I moved into a rented flat I could work through my feelings without anyone watching and have a good wallow until I'd got over Tom.

That was the plan, anyway.

Ben insists that I had a breakdown; I'm not sure if he's right, all I know is that I struggled and yes, I did do some things that I don't remember doing. The rambling texts that I sent to Tom – according to Tom – sounded as if I was suicidal. Tom contacted Ben and totally panicked him and with Mum away on holiday and unable to check on me, he drove down from London at break-neck speed to find me passed out on the sofa. I'd done my usual night-time routine of drinking half a bottle of wine to help me sleep – but it didn't mix well with the anti-depressants. I wasn't suicidal but I don't blame Ben for thinking that I was and I soon discovered that sending texts was my go-to behaviour after a couple of glasses of wine. Several of mine and Tom's joint friends received bitter texts from me that I would never have sent if I'd been sober. Once I'd apologised our friends said that they understood because of the state I was in but once something has been said, it can't be unsaid no matter that you didn't mean it. And some of those texts were pretty nasty. I realised that anti-depressants weren't the answer and did what I should have done in the first place; I stopped taking the tablets and grieved for the love and life that I'd lost. I also stopped drinking; I'd started using wine to help myself sleep and kidded myself that a few glasses every night wouldn't hurt. After the Ben intervention I was honest with myself – alcohol is a slippery slope and not one that I wanted to go hurtling down.

So with all that happened then I should have learned my lesson but I haven't; because I've slipped back into the habit of having a couple of glasses of wine in the evening to help myself sleep.

But it's going to stop.

I fling back the duvet and haul myself out of bed; time to get back to normal. No more drinking, no more dwelling on things and no more making excuses for not getting on with life. Diana has been dealt with and it's time to move on.

I march purposefully to the bathroom and turn the shower on full blast.

Time to wake up.

*　*　*

After ten minutes under a hot shower I feel immeasurably better and by the time I'm dressed I'm feeling much brighter. I give the duvet a good shake and haul it over the end of the bed to air.

I open the bedroom window wide to let in some fresh air and look outside at the sunshine. We've had mostly lovely weather since May apart from a few odd days where it's rained and today looks like it's going to be good again. I take several deep breaths of air and remind myself that it's great to be alive; I'm reasonably young, fit, healthy and solvent and I have my whole life ahead of me. Maybe I'll take up running or some other sort of sport. I have no desire to go back to the gym but there must be some form of exercise that I can enjoy. I'll give it some thought – I could even buy a bike.

Positive, mental attitude is all I need.

I'm going to make a definite date with Phoebe to go to the drama club with her and I'm going to stick to it. I've put it off long enough. It's time to move on properly; I keep on saying I'll go next week and I never do. The Diana episode has blighted the last few weeks but no more; it's over and done with and I'm not going to waste anymore time thinking about it. As I come down the stairs I can feel a cold draft on my arms and I wonder if I should go back up and close my bedroom window a bit; maybe it's not as warm outside as I think.

I halt in my tracks as I walk into the kitchen.

The back door is wide open and the source of the draft that I felt on the stairs. My stomach flips over and my hand flies to my mouth. My house has been broken into and I never even heard it happen. A quick glance around the room confirms that nothing appears to have been disturbed – not surprising as there's not much to steal from a kitchen; a thief is hardly going to ransack the food cupboards. I run into the dining room; there's also nothing to actually steal in here, just a table and four chairs. I continue into the lounge with a sinking heart expecting to see that the television has gone and the room has been turned upside down in a search for valuables. I don't have a huge amount of possessions but those I have I value, and the thought of someone ransacking my home whilst I was fast asleep fills me with horror. What if they'd come upstairs? Nightmare scenarios start to fill my head and I shake them away; there's no need to get in a state now because thankfully, that didn't happen.

The television stares back at me and the room looks exactly the same as always. I turn and go back out to the kitchen and over to the back door. I search for signs of damage around the doorframe or door but I can't see any. When I swing the door closed I see that the key is in the lock on the inside, which can only mean one thing.

I opened it myself.

CHAPTER TWENTY

Did I open the door and forget that I'd done so?

I must have.

The door was unlocked from the inside and now that Diana no longer has a key that only leaves one person who could have done this.

Me.

I think back to last night and I can't actually remember going to bed. I obviously did go to bed but I have no clear recollection of doing so no matter how hard I try to remember. I must have opened the back door for some reason and left it open – definitely not a good thing to do. Maybe I went out to the dustbin; I concentrate and try to remember but it's a blank. It's fortunate that I don't smoke or else I could have burned the house down with a discarded cigarette.

Did I drink more than I thought? Because two glasses of wine shouldn't have made me so drunk that I can't remember going to bed.

No. I know that I *definitely* only drank two glasses of wine because that's all I allow myself and there's still a half empty bottle still standing on the draining board where I left it. Alcohol seems to affect me far more than it used to; Tom and I used to drink on a regular basis and in those days two glasses of wine would have had hardly any effect on me. Meals out at the weekend always involved alcohol and a stressful day at work was always a good excuse to open a bottle of wine in the evening. It's only in the last couple of weeks that I've started drinking wine again but it's been so long that I've lost my tolerance for it, two glasses now has the effect of making me sleepy and fuzzy headed.

Which is the reason why I've been drinking every evening; it helps me fall into a deep sleep – albeit sleep that's disturbed by bizarre dreams.

I've been very lucky this time; the door was wide open last night and anyone could have come in and murdered me in my bed or ransacked the house. It's only the fact that I have a fenced off back garden that has stopped a casual thief from spotting a lucky opportunity to rob my house. Imagine if it was the front door I'd left open? I shudder at the thought of what could have happened.

My mobile phone is lying on the kitchen worktop on charge where I left it last night – that would most certainly be gone. I pick my phone up and it's completely dead; I must have forgotten to actually turn the charger on. I flick the switch to put it on charge and then fill the kettle and put it on to boil. This is a wake-up call; I intended stopping the wine drinking anyway but this has made it imperative that I do so. No more drinking.

At all.

I tip some cornflakes into a bowl and slosh milk over them. I just have time to bolt them down and still get to the mini market on time. I spoon instant coffee into a mug and decide to have it black; I need the kick of caffeine that it will give me. I pour the boiling water into the mug and then top it up with tap water to cool it. I could easily forgo breakfast as I have no appetite but I have a sickly feeling in my stomach from the wine and I need to line it with something. I scoop up a spoonful of cornflakes and ram them into my mouth whilst trying to slip my shoes on at the same time. Sourness hits my throat and I lean over the sink and spit the cornflakes out into the sink. The milk is off; really off. I look at the bowl and the milk is curdled in lumps around the cornflakes. I gag and clamp my hand over my mouth and then quickly glug down a glass of water, swiftly followed by a mouthful of coffee to take away the foul taste.

I don't have time to have anything else for breakfast now but I don't think I could face eating anything now. Before I leave the house I take the milk carton back out of the fridge and pour the remaining milk down the sink. I try not to gag as I run the water to disperse the lumps down the plughole. I can't believe that it's gone off so badly overnight; I used this milk only yesterday and it was fine. As I'm about to chuck the empty carton into the bin I check the date on the rim; it's over three weeks ago.

How can this be possible?

I buy milk in two pint cartons because I don't use a huge amount. I last bought some on Saturday and I *always* check the date before I buy. This must be an old carton that I left in the fridge and I've used it instead of the new one.

I pull open the fridge door and check; there is no other carton anywhere. I couldn't have bought any milk on Saturday; I obviously had it in my mind to buy some but didn't actually do it. I'm *sure* that I bought milk but I couldn't have, could I? I can see myself doing it but that must have been on another day.

I don't have time to dwell on it now so I gulp down the last of my coffee, grab my jacket and leave the house. I make sure to be fully aware that I lock the front door properly instead of doing it on automatic pilot; I even come back and check when I've got to the gate to make doubly sure that it's locked.

I march to work briskly and purposefully as if this will convince me that I'm not getting forgetful or doing things without realising that I've done them. I know what I'm doing, I tell myself but the thought is there and refuses to budge.

If I can't rely on my own memory then what else could I have done?

* * *

By the time I get to the mini market I'm determined to forget about last night and start as I mean to go on. It's gone off milk, for God's sake, there's no need to have a breakdown over it. Yes, I did leave the back door open which is definitely not good but I've learned my lesson; no more wine for me. It's time to get on with my life and today I'm going to arrange to go to drama club with Phoebe later in the week; she sent me a picture of the latest play last week to try and tempt me to audition but I put her off again with a lame excuse. This week I'm actually going to say yes and do it; if I'm too late to audition then I'll just have to paint scenery or make cups of tea or anything else that needs doing. I need to get out and enjoy life, not sit indoors on my own in the evenings drinking wine. I'm also going to make a start on my up-cycling; I haven't done any renovating since doing my own table and chairs and I seem to have let all my good intentions slip. I intend to rectify that this week. I'm sure that there'll be something suitable to up-cycle on the second hand furniture for sale on Facebook and I can make it my first project. Anything will do, even if it's small; I can then either sell it myself or approach one of the boutique furniture shops in town and see if they're interested. Pre-loved shops seem to be popping up all over the place and several months ago I popped into two shops and asked if they'd be interested and one of them said they'd take a look at what I have to offer and take it from there.

I feel more positive and optimistic as I push open the door to the shop and I give Phoebe a cheery wave as she stands at the till serving a customer. My brisk marching has worked and I've arrived with five minutes to spare. I go through to the back office and hang my handbag on the hook and come back out in to the shop.

'Morning Phoebe,' I trill as the remaining customer disappears through the door and out onto the street. Phoebe doesn't answer as she closes the till and comes round from behind the counter to let me through.

'I didn't think you'd be in,' she says, unsmilingly.

I feel my own smile slip and I try to ignore the hollow feeling in my stomach.

'Why?' I ask. 'What made you think that?'

'You made it quite clear what you think of this shop,' Phoebe says, grimly. 'And me.'

'What do you mean?' I ask.

'Your texts. Last night.'

I watch silently as Phoebe pulls her mobile phone out of her pocket and taps the screen.

'Remember now?' she asks as she holds the screen up in front of my face and I see a screen full of texts from my number. They're horrible;

vile language saying that I must have been mad to take a job here and that she needs to stop pestering me to be a friend because why would I want to be friends with a saddo like her. And more; much more and much worse. My stomach churns and I swallow hard, afraid that I'm going to vomit.

'Phoebe,' I flounder, unable to believe that this nightmare is happening again. 'Honestly, you have to believe me, I didn't send those texts. It wasn't me, that's not what I think of you at all.'

'Really?' Phoebe glares at me and I realise that I've never seen her angry before but she certainly looks angry now.

'So who was it then?' she asks. 'Because it came from your phone so who else could it possibly be?'

CHAPTER TWENTY-ONE

I trudge home feeling the worst that I've ever felt – and I include when Tom and I split up in that statement. I may have been heartbroken then but I never doubted my own sanity. I'm facing the almost certain fact that I've been doing things without knowing; that I am in fact, seriously mentally ill.

I'm terrified of what I might do next.

This morning has been beyond awful and although I stayed the morning in the mini market and worked my shift. I think that Phoebe would have been happier if I'd not bothered and left immediately. I tried to convince her that I never sent the horrible texts but I had no explanation as to who *had* sent them. I could tell that she didn't believe me.

I don't believe me.

I didn't have my phone on me as I'd left it at home charging, but as Phoebe held her screen up to me I managed to check the time the messages were sent.

It was eleven-forty-five last night.

It can only have been me.

I was at home alone and there was no one else with me so only I had access to my phone. I can choose to believe that Diana hacked my Facebook account and that she made the comments to Tom, but is it even possible to send texts from somewhere else other than the phone they appear to come from? I think it unlikely; I think it more likely that I sent them myself and if that is so, then I must have put the messages to Tom on Facebook as well.

I cannot even remember what time I went to bed so how can I know that I didn't send Phoebe the texts?

I can't; because there is no one else who *could* have sent them.

I have history for texting when drunk but I always assumed that true feelings were supposed to emerge when drunk. The messages to Phoebe were horrible but I honestly don't feel that way about her so why would I send them? They don't even sound like me. I haven't known Phoebe for very long but I think she's a great person and I value her friendship so why on earth would I send such texts to her? I also love working in the mini market so it doesn't make any sort of sense; it's almost as if I'm trying to sabotage myself.

I'd already decided that I wasn't going to drink anymore but that has just confirmed that I need to stop immediately. I've decided that I'm going to make an appointment to see a doctor; I don't feel stressed but whatever is wrong with me is making me do odd, out of character things and I need help before I do something even worse. I haven't been sleeping well and all those weird dreams that I've been having must have a reason. The break up with Tom has left its mark; I thought I was over it but I obviously have issues that haven't been resolved; perhaps I need counselling. I won't have anti-depressants again because they made me like a zombie last time but whatever other help is available, I'll take it.

Decision made; I'm going to make an appointment – but before I do that I'm going to ring Ben because I need to hear a friendly voice again. What's happened this morning with Phoebe has shaken me to the core and I've been fighting back the tears for the last four hours. My new life is crumbling around me and aside from making an appointment to see a doctor, I don't know what else to do. Ben's on my side; no matter what I've done I know that my brother always has my back so I'm going to tell him everything and ask him for help.

I've walked home on automatic pilot and arrived home without even realising it; I can't remember anything about the walk and feel as if I am elsewhere. If I can walk home without having any memory of it that just proves that anything is possible. I open the front gate and walk up the path to my front door just in time to see Bert hurriedly going into his own house.

He obviously saw me coming and is doing his best to avoid me and who can blame him?

I swallow down the lump in my throat and root around in my jacket pocket for my keys. I pull out the keys, unlock the front door and let myself into the house and then close and lock the front door behind me although God knows why; the only person I need to be afraid of is myself.

I walk through the hallway to the kitchen and as I toss the keys onto the worktop I notice that there's a screwed up till receipt caught on the key ring. I pull it off and am about to chuck it into the bin when something stops me. I unravel the receipt and lay it on the worktop and smooth the creases out as best I can. The receipt is dated for Saturday and it's from the mini Tesco's just around the corner from Mum's apartment. I called in there on my way home after I'd popped in for a coffee with her and that's when I thought that I'd bought milk. I only picked up a few things and the receipt shows what I bought.

A pack of wholemeal rolls, a chocolate bar.

And two pints of milk.

* * *

I haven't moved for over an hour; I'm still sitting at the dining room table, receipt in hand, staring at it. I'm clutching onto the crumpled receipt as if it's a lifeline because it's the only proof I have that I'm not going insane. But even though this proves that I *did* buy some milk, I still can't make any sense of what's happening. I stare at the receipt in the futile hope that it is somehow going to provide me with some answers.

Maybe it can.

It proves that I *did* buy milk on Saturday, as I originally thought, and that I didn't imagine doing so. The empty milk carton on the table in front of me is not the one that I bought on Saturday, it's the one that I've retrieved from the kitchen bin where I threw it this morning. The carton is not a Tesco's one and, what's more, I *know* that I never bought it at all.

How do I know this?

Because it isn't from a shop that I go to; it's from the Co-op. I didn't notice that fact this morning because I was in a rush and actually, I had no reason to look at it properly. The colours are the same as the milk that the mini market sells so I assumed that I must have bought it from there, but I didn't.

Could I have bought it from the Co-op without realising, the same way that I sent the messages to Phoebe? Could I have travelled to the co-op and completely forgotten?

No.

Because I don't even *know* where the Co-op

supermarket is; but more to the point, the milk was bought when I was working my shift at the mini market so it's impossible for me to have bought it myself.

Which convinces me of something else.

I didn't send the text messages either.

The relief that I felt when I realised this was immense; I was moved to tears by the fact that I'm not going mad and have no need to doubt my own sanity. When Phoebe showed me the texts this morning I felt the worst that I've ever felt in my life because the proof was there that I'd been living another life parallel to my own that I knew nothing about.

But now I know; the messages don't sound like me because they're not me; I did not send them. Somehow, Diana has been in here and done these things and I have no idea how or why. But how, how is she getting in? Her key will no longer fit the lock and there is no way she can have the keys to my new locks so how is it possible?

I have no idea but I'm going to find out and put a stop to her.

I get up from the table and go out into the kitchen and stare out of the window into the back garden. I should eat; my stomach feels hollow and I have the beginnings of a sickly headache but the thought of food is unappealing. I feel jumpy and unsettled and wish that there was some action I could take that would stop all of this madness. I'm beyond relieved that I'm *not* having some sort of a breakdown but the downside to that is that I have a psychotic neighbour who is trying to destroy me and I don't know why. Perhaps Jayne is right; maybe I should leave immediately and never come back; sell the house and start afresh somewhere else before she totally ruins my life.

My gaze settles on the half-empty bottle of wine on the draining board and deciding to take decisive action on something that I *can* change, I pick the bottle up and unscrew the top and tip the remaining contents into the sink. I watch the liquid glug down the plughole and when the bottle is empty I'm about to turn on the tap to rinse it away when I notice something odd; as the last sputter of wine leaves the bottle something else comes out with it.

Fine, white, powdery sediment.

CHAPTER TWENTY-TWO

I climb down from the chair and then pick it up and take it back into the dining room and tuck it neatly underneath the table. That was the very last kitchen cupboard to search and, as I suspected, I didn't find what I was looking for. I remember when I moved in that I never put anything in the top cupboard because it was too high to reach easily but to settle my mind, I had to look.

So, now I know for sure.

The white sediment at the bottom of the wine bottle was, I'm certain, the residue of my crushed up anti-depressant tablets. Although I only took them for a short while I never threw the ones that were left in the packets away. I put them with the assorted painkillers, indigestion tablets, plasters and other vaguely medical bits into a plastic box which I keep in the kitchen cupboard above the cups and mugs. I had no intention of ever taking them again, but I definitely did keep them because I didn't feel that I could just throw drugs into the dustbin along with the household rubbish. I had intended on doing the responsible thing and taking them to the pharmacy to dispose of but never got around to it. They've been languishing in that plastic box for nearly a year.

But now I cannot find them anywhere.

The wooziness and strange dreams that have been affecting me now make perfect sense; drinking two glasses of wine in the evening didn't make me feel like that.

Wine laced with anti-depressants caused it.

My next door neighbour has been poisoning me.

It sounds completely mad but there is no other explanation for it. Somehow, Diana has been in my house and sent the text messages to Phoebe but I have no idea how she's still able to get in. Whilst I'm in the house I'll make sure to push the bolts across the front and back doors so that even if she has somehow obtained a key to my new lock she won't be able get in.

But I don't see *how* she can have a key.

It's not possible.

But somehow, it is, because there is no other way.

* * *

I went upstairs to bed, late, and made sure to take

my mobile phone with me in case somehow, Diana somehow gets in here. The thought of her prowling around my house whilst I sleep makes me feel sick to my stomach because if she can drug me, who knows what else she could do. I console myself with the thought that both doors are bolted so even with a key she won't be able to get through them. All evening I've see-sawed between ringing Ben and telling him everything that's been happening, or not ringing him and only telling him when I have incontrovertible proof – although what that proof would be, I have no idea. The fact that he didn't believe me when I voiced my fears to him about Diana still hurts; what if he still doubts me? Quite honestly, if someone told me this was happening to them, I don't think I would believe it. I have no proof of anything and the whole thing sounds completely crazy and as if I'm imagining things and going insane. No, I'm not going to tell him until I can prove what she's been doing.

By the time I went to bed I thought there was no possibility at all that I would be able to sleep; I felt on edge and totally wired but physically exhausted. I'd made myself eat some pizza for dinner as I hadn't eaten a thing all day but it tasted as if I was chewing cardboard and I had to force it down. I followed it with two cups of black tea, which was pretty vile, and tried to forget about the fresh bottle of wine that was sitting in the fridge just waiting to be drunk. Despite the promise that I'd made to myself about not drinking, I was tempted to have a couple of glasses to help me sleep. I could have some now, I told myself, because Diana couldn't have tampered with the bottle in the fridge because it hadn't been opened.

Which set me thinking; how had she managed to do it, because I've felt the same grogginess and disturbed sleep every night but how could a fresh bottle of wine have anti-depressants in it? I felt compelled to go out to the fridge and check, promising myself that there was no way I was going to drink any of it. I got the new bottle out of the fridge and examined the screw top closely. And there it was; the faintest gap between the bottle top and the seal, the merest fraction bigger than it should have been. The top had been screwed back on tightly and unless I'd been looking for it I wouldn't have seen it.

And of course I was never looking for it.

I tipped the contents of the bottle down the sink and then threw it in the recycling bin. There was no point in keeping it as evidence because I have no proof that Diana had been in and laced it with the anti-depressants because who's to say that I hadn't done it myself? No one will believe me because I didn't believe Jayne, I thought she was paranoid.

All of these thoughts were whizzing around in my head as I got into bed and I almost went back downstairs to watch television as I couldn't see that there was any possibility of getting to sleep. But somehow, I did fall asleep and when I woke this morning it was to the aftermath of more bizarre dreams – although the grogginess and fuzziness wasn't so bad. I guess this was because I'm not longer being drugged.

Drugged.

It sounds completely mad; it *is* completely mad.

She is completely mad.

The thought of a psychotic next door neighbour is not good but infinitely better than being mad or psychotic myself. For a while I couldn't trust myself, I couldn't trust what I might be capable of. At least I know that I'm not the one of unsound mind.

Once I'd showered and dressed, I came downstairs and the bolts were still across the front and back door so she couldn't have come in whilst I was asleep. Maybe, I told myself, I've stopped her now.

But I can't bring myself to completely believe that.

I didn't bother with having breakfast or even a cup of tea; this was because I have no milk, I told myself. But a part of me knows that the real reason is because I was afraid; I was afraid to open my own fridge and discover that there was something in there that I hadn't put there myself. I can try to convince myself that I'm not afraid but why did I sleep with my mobile phone underneath my pillow last night? Perhaps Ben is right; maybe I should go and stay with Mum for a while.

But why should I? It's my house, not hers, and I won't allow her to drive me away.

I could have stayed off work and maybe Phoebe

would rather I did as things are so awkward between us at the moment, but I didn't; because then Diana will have won. I won't allow her to ruin my life and I won't allow her to reduce me to a nervous wreck like she's done to Jayne. I was forced out of my home by Tom and his secretary and I won't be dictated to again. So I made myself spend an uncomfortable morning in the mini market with Phoebe being icily polite to me whilst I pretended that everything was okay between us. It was embarrassing and uncomfortable and I stopped myself many times from trying to tell her what's been happening – because why on earth would she believe me? If I want to salvage anything from our friendship I'm going to have to lie and tell her that I've had a breakdown or I'm suffering from stress because that is the only believable explanation. A nightmare, insane next door neighbour trying to poison me is not.

It's a relief to get away from the cold atmosphere when my shift finally ends and I try to convince myself that things will get better once Phoebe has calmed down. My nerves are in shreds and as I walk home the sound of a car back-firing makes me physically jump. In that instant the dream that I woke to this morning comes flooding back to me and I remember it vividly. I know with sudden clarity that I've had this dream many times over the last few weeks and it stops me in my tracks as I cross the road. It's only when a car horn honks at me that I realise I've stopped in the middle of the road to try and make sense of what I've just re-membered. I hurriedly step onto the pavement and stand and take a deep breath to steady myself.

In that split second of clarity it all became crys-tal clear and I understood the significance of the dreams.

They were telling me how Diana's getting into my house.

CHAPTER
TWENTY-THREE

Mobile phone in hand, I gaze up at the loft hatch. I haven't been up in the loft at all since I moved in. I made a promise to myself that I was going to start as I meant to go on and not shove stuff up there and fill it up with old junk that should really go straight into the dustbin. Tom and I used to do just such a thing; old clothes, things that we didn't use any more but were too good to throw out, ornaments and old books that should have gone straight to the charity shop or rubbish tip were shied up in the loft, out of sight and out of mind. And there it stayed until the loft was so full that we couldn't fit anything else up there. We then had to have a big clear out and take car loads of it all to the council tip – which is where we should have taken it in the first place.

When I viewed the house the Estate Agent made

sure to tell me that the loft hatch has its own integral step ladder for ease of access and what a great place it was for storage. He made a big selling point of this but I remember dismissing what he was saying as I had no intention of ever using it. Looking at it now, it may have its own ladder but the loft hatch is still far too close to the top of the stairs for my liking. I have an aversion to heights and don't relish the thought of balancing on a step ladder to try and clamber into the loft with the chasm of the stairs below me.

Aware that time is ticking by, I tuck my phone into my jeans pocket and ready myself. I have no idea if there is lighting up there so I'll have to use the torch on my phone but I'm not relishing the thought of clambering around in a dank, dark, loft. I take a deep breath and hold up the long pole with a hook on the end that I found in the built-in wardrobe in the spare bedroom. I manoeuvre the hook into the circular metal ring in the middle of the hatch door and pull.

Nothing happens.

I yank it a bit harder but nothing moves. I grip the pole tightly with both hands and using all my strength and weight, I pull downwards as hard as I can. There's a screech of metal and I have to jump smartly backwards as the hatch flies open and a metal ladder comes clattering out of the loft towards me, knocking the pole clean out of my hands. I realise that I've gone about it all wrong; I was standing on the wrong side of the hatch. If I'd stood on the other side to pull it open it wouldn't have required such force. Perhaps I should have paid more attention to the estate agent when he demonstrated it. I stare at the ladder and imagine Diana climbing down it in the middle of the night; how could I not have heard her?

But I did hear her; in my drug and alcohol induced sleep I dreamed of furniture being moved around upstairs, of people marching above me, of thunder and lightning raining down on me. The clues were all there but I couldn't make sense of them. I'm guessing that I must have been at work the first time she came in through the loft hatch so she had no need to be quiet. Besides, she would have done it many times before when Jayne lived here.

Enough dwelling on what's gone before; I need to get up there and have a look.

I clamber up the rungs and try to ignore the looming stairwell below me and the vision of my body plummeting downwards into the hallway. Diana obviously has no fear of heights if she can climb down this step ladder in total darkness and be sure of where she's going. Although maybe she turned the lights on – because would I have even been aware if she had?

Once up in the loft I sit on the side of the hatch and pull my phone out of my pocket and click the torch on. I point it upwards and gaze up at the roof but can see no sign of a light hanging anywhere. I pan the torch around and it illuminates old cardboard boxes and several mounds that look like piles of clothes. My mind is working overtime and I shake off the thought that there's a body underneath one of them. I pull my legs up through the hatch and swing them around and then shine my torch down at the floor. The spaces between the joists have been filled with fibreboard and I'm relieved that I don't have to balance across the joists to make my way across. I crawl on hands and knees – thankful that I'm wearing jeans – towards the wall between my house and Diana's, unable to stand up as the roof is not high enough. The air is still and there's a tropical, humid feel to the atmosphere.

I'm beginning to wonder if I could have got it wrong when I spot it; a subtle difference in the pattern of the bricks in the left corner of the loft. I point the beam of my phone torch directly at it and screw my eyes up and squint. I can see that the outline of the bricks definitely changes to a smoother, darker surface. It would be unnoticeable if I wasn't looking for it.

I crawl towards the corner, avoiding the boxes and a large pile of discarded sheets and blankets and stop in front of the wall and shine the torch around. I can see now that the bricks have been removed and the smooth surface is something blocking the hole from the other side, maybe a piece of board or wood. This is proof enough of how she's getting in but I need to be absolutely certain. I push my hand against whatever is covering the hole on the other side of the wall. Fully expecting to meet resistance, I'm shocked when the board falls away from my hand and the hole is revealed.

The hole is easily big enough to crawl through and I crouch forward and point the beam of my phone through the hole and it illuminates Diana's loft. Unlike mine, Diana's loft doesn't appear to have boarding between the joists but I can see that a thin line of boards has been laid from the loft hatch to the hole in the wall to crawl across. I try to picture Diana clambering through the hole; she's tall and thickset so it can't be an easy task. I also ask myself the question that I've asked myself so many times before, yet am still unable to find an answer to.

Why?

She must derive some sort of enjoyment from it because why else would she bother? She must have done the same when Jayne lived here and I wonder if she drugged her too. My next door neighbour is beyond deranged; I thought that she had earmarked me for this treatment because I gave her the cold shoulder but I now realise that it wouldn't matter, because she doesn't need a reason. Even if I'd done her tax return as she demanded there would have come a time when I fell foul of her; I feel sure that she would have pushed me to the limit to give herself a reason to turn against me.

She's quite mad.

Jayne's words come back to me and I shudder.

If you want your life back, you'll have to kill me first.

I shake the thought away and crawl through the hole and into her loft; the pile of bricks that she's removed from the wall are neatly piled up next to the hole. Sitting on the top of the bricks is a small box; my missing anti-depressants. I pick them up and take out the inner foils to see how many are left. I was prescribed three months worth but stopped taking them after less than a month.

There are only a handful left.

She's drugged me with nearly two months worth of pills in a few weeks. I wonder now how I was able to function as well as I did; no wonder I felt paranoid and doubted myself at every turn. It's a miracle that I could function at all. What would she drug me with when they'd run out? Did she plan to kill me and make it look like an overdose? Was that her plan for Jayne, too?

I can't think about that now; all I know is that I have to make sure that she can never get into my house again. I'm going to call out a carpenter or handyman to come and seal up my loft hatch so that it can never be opened again. In the meantime I'll padlock the hatch closed somehow until it can be done permanently.

I put the foils back into the box and stuff it into my jeans pocket. I resume my onward crawl and carefully inch my way along the narrow boarding towards Diana's loft hatch but come to a stop midway. What do I think I'm going to find – a signed confession? The hole in the wall proves nothing; nothing that would stand up in a court of law, anyway. All I've done is confirm to myself that I'm not mad and that Diana is; I've no need to go any further, once my loft hatch is sealed there is no other way she can get into my house.

Or I could sell up as Jayne suggested because will Diana ever stop? If I stop her getting in this way will she find another? I can't think about it now; whether I want to continue living next door to a madwoman is a decision for another time, not now. For now I need to go back into my own house and make sure that the loft is no longer an accessible route for her. I'll go and buy myself a chain and padlock as a temporary measure; if I pull the chain through the hook in the hatch door I can anchor the chain to the stair banister and secure it with a padlock. Not very elegant but it'll do for now.

I take a last look around Diana's loft which looks very much like mine – discarded boxes of junk, only hers are balanced across the joists – and then twist around carefully on the narrow board to make my way back towards my own. I'm crawling my way towards the hole when I hear the unmistakable, distant, sound of a front door opening and closing.

Diana's home.

I glance at the torch on my phone and tell myself not to panic; there's no way that she can know that I'm up here because she's on the ground floor and I'm all the way up here in the loft. There's no reason for her to suspect that I know how she's been getting in because I told her myself that I knew she had a key; how she must have secretly laughed at me.

Nevertheless, my heart is pounding like a train as I slowly crawl towards the hole in the wall. The air is humid and warm and I feel a bead of sweat slowly trickle down my face. It's slow going trying to crawl with the phone in my hand and, eager to reach the safety of my own home, I attempt to speed up.

Which is when my mobile phone slips from my sweating fingers.

And lands with a resounding thud between the joists.

CHAPTER TWENTY-FOUR

I hold my breath and carefully retrieve my phone from between the rafters. Surely Diana can't have heard; she's on the ground floor and a long way from the loft.

Although the house is silent so maybe it sounded really loud.

It's too bad; in a few minutes I'll be gone from here and safely back in my own home.

Except it's not safe; she can still get in.

Telling myself to stop faffing around and being ridiculous I scramble along the boarding, forcing myself to take my time so that I don't drop my phone again. I'm a foot away from the hole in the wall when I hear movement behind me. I turn my head to see Diana's loft hatch opening; seconds later her head emerges through the gap.

'Caught you!' she shouts loudly in an almost

jolly manner.

I stare at her for a moment and then resume my crawl across the boards. A few more shuffles and I'll be through the hole and I can get to my feet and run doubled-over to the loft hatch. Once I'm back in my house I'll have to do something to stop her following. I have no idea what but I'll think of something. If I poke the hook through the ring on the hatch and put all of my weight behind it she won't be able to get it open.

'How dare you come onto my property!' she shouts

I turn to see that she's sitting on the side of the hatch and she's hauling her legs through the gap and into the loft.

'You needn't think you'll get away with it!' She shouts as she points the beam of a large torch straight into my eyes.

The light blinds me and I cover my eyes with my hand. I want to laugh at the cheek of her but fear gets the better of me; I'm not sure why I'm so afraid of her but despite being younger than her she's much taller and larger than me and I don't relish the thought of physical contact with her. I've never had a fight in my life and I don't want to start now by exchanging blows with a deranged woman in the confines of a loft. I don't fancy getting bashed over the head by the huge torch that she's waving around, either. I turn away from her and scramble through the hole into my own loft and rise to my feet, ready to make a crouching run towards the loft hatch. I start to move forward but in my haste to get away I don't bend over quite far enough and I catch the top of my head against the rafters. The unexpected pain is excruciating and I see stars for a moment but I carry on moving forward; no way am I getting stuck up here with Diana.

I reach the loft opening and lower myself through the hole and have my foot on the bottom rung of the ladder when an ear-piercing scream reverberates from above. It's followed by a crashing, explosive bang and a thud that seems to shake the entire house.

Then silence.

I pause, frozen, almost afraid to go back up the ladder to see what's happened. I'm almost sure that Diana has missed her footing on the narrow boards between the joists and fallen through the loft floor between them.

I should go back up and help her, she must be injured.

I have a mini argument with myself; don't help, she doesn't deserve it, the nasty part of me says; serves her right. Even as I'm telling myself this I know that ignoring her is not an option; there's no way I can leave her lying injured with possible broken bones even if I wanted to; it's simply not in my nature. I'm going to have to go and see if she's okay.

I clamber back up the ladder into the loft and crouch-run back across the loft and wriggle through the hole in the wall. I immediately see that there's a huge hole between two joists; as I suspected, Diana has fallen through it. I wince at the thought of her crashing through the ceiling because she's not a small person and it must have been a tight fit between the joists as she went down.

I inch my way across the boards to her loft hatch and carefully climb down the ladder to the landing. As I look around me I regret my haste to come and help her as I cannot see Diana anywhere. Plaster and broken pieces of timber litter the landing but Diana is nowhere to be seen. She's obviously not as badly injured as I suspected and has no doubt dusted herself off and will appear any moment. I'm now alone in her house with her and no one even knows that I'm here. I curse my stupidity and naivety at putting myself in danger through my misguided good Samaritan act. In Diana's state of mind who knows what she might do, if she can poison me who knows what else she's capable of? She's hardly going to be friendly towards me now, is she? I hurriedly turn and grab hold of the ladder and am attempting to scramble back up into the loft as quickly as possible when I see her.

The reason she's not on the landing is because she's in the downstairs hallway. She's lying spread-eagled on her back, her arms and legs flung wide, starfish style, with her head at an awkward angle. From my viewpoint at the top of the stairs she doesn't appear to be moving and I don't think that she's conscious. I look up at the ceiling to see that the hole from the loft is directly above the stairs and there would have been nothing to break her fall; she would have crashed straight through the ceiling and plummeted down the stairs.

I climb down the ladder onto the landing and carefully pick my way through the debris of plaster and wood and make my way down the stairs. When I reach the hallway I kneel down beside Diana and place my fingers on her wrist to feel for her pulse. I soon realise that this is completely pointless as I can't feel anything except for my own heart pounding erratically. I'm not even sure if I know *how* to feel for someone's pulse so I need to think what to do. I have a vague recollection from a first aid course many years ago that the airway should be protected at all costs. She's on her back so should I turn her over into the recovery position? I could, but if she's injured her spine that may be the very worst thing that I could do; what if moving her causes more damage?

There is only one sensible course of action; ring for an ambulance immediately and let the experts tend to her. I turn the torch off on my phone and flick through to the telephone keypad. I've already keyed in the first two nines when I look down and see that Diana is staring unwaveringly at me.

I jump backwards in horror, nearly toppling over as I do so. I steady myself and then quickly realise that of course Diana is not staring at me.

She's dead.

Her head is twisted to one side at an impossible

angle, her chest is not moving at all because she's not breathing and her eyes are staring unseeingly. I assume by the position of her head that she's broken her neck. I'm almost certain that she's dead but feel that I should check so, knowing that it's impossible to know if I've found the right place to check for a pulse, I hold the screen of my phone close to her mouth. When I check it after what seems like forever, the screen hasn't misted at all,

She's not breathing.

I take the screen away from her mouth and turn it around and am about to tap in the last number nine for the emergency services when I pause. I move away from Diana and sit on the bottom step of the stairs and consider the situation.

I've no idea how long I sit there but eventually I reach a decision. I hold my phone up and carefully delete the two nines and slowly tuck the phone into my pocket.

CHAPTER TWENTY-FIVE

I apologised to Phoebe this morning for the vile texts that I sent her; I told her that I'm not making excuses for my behaviour but that I've done things that I have no knowledge of doing. I said that the anti-depressants that I'd been taking had not mixed well with the wine that I'd started drinking to help me sleep.

I tried very hard not to sound as if I was asking for sympathy or excusing my behaviour in any way but more that I was being open and honest. I told her that I have no idea why I texted those horrible messages to her because it's not the way that I think about her at all. I told her that I valued her friendship more than she could ever know but that I would quite understand if she wanted nothing more to do with me. Quite honestly, I wasn't sure that she would accept my apology but I felt that I had to at least try. I also told her that I had arranged some counselling for myself through the doctor's surgery so that I could get the help that I very obviously need.

Once I'd finished with my story, Phoebe surprised me by seeming relieved that we could draw a line underneath it all and try and get back to some sort of normality. Obviously, things aren't going to be the same but I'm hopeful that with time, we can resume our friendship properly. I was fully prepared for her to rebuff my apology and I wouldn't have blamed her at all if she had. Had she done so I fully intended giving my notice in and finding a job elsewhere.

So, things are looking up, and whilst I didn't have a spring in my step on my walk home after my shift, I definitely felt lighter and more optimistic than I did before I left this morning. As I turned the corner into my street I half expected to see an ambulance outside Diana's house but of course there wasn't, because no one, except me, knows that she's dead.

I haven't told anyone what happened and nor will I; this will be a secret that will never be told.

After I'd made the decision not to ring the emergency services I sat with Diana's body for quite a while. I repeated the phone test several times to make absolutely sure that she was dead, although from the angle of her head she'd clearly broken her neck. I'm usually the most squeamish person alive and would never have thought that I could sit by a dead body and be so unbothered by it. Even when my own father died I refused to go and see him at the chapel of rest as I was afraid that he would look different and I would never be able to remember him as he really was.

I'm actually a little shocked at my own callousness; I'm not saying that I'm glad she's dead but in all honesty, I can't say that I'm sorry. When I think of Jayne's terror and what she'd done to her and what Diana did to me, I can't help thinking that the world is a better place without her.

The worst thing that Diana did was to make me doubt my own sanity.

I realise that things would only have got worse; she had no qualms about coming into my house and doing exactly as she wished and although I had stopped her coming in through the loft, I'm certain that she would have found another way to destroy me. It occurred to me as I was sitting next to her body that the only way she could have used my mobile phone was to use the face recognition feature to open it. There's no way she could have guessed the pass code and although I assumed she'd hacked my Facebook account elsewhere, she had no need to; she would have simply used my phone.

She drugged me and held a phone over my face whilst I slept. What sort of person does that? Not a normal one, that's for sure. Pretty much my whole life is on that phone – the banking app uses face recognition as does my email and everything else.

She could easily have ruined me and I've no doubt that she fully intended to. The thought of her watching me as I was sleeping makes me shudder. What would she have done if I'd woken up and seen her? She drugged me with anti-depressants without a qualm so what else would she have been capable of? Would it have been a bang over the head to silence me? A pillow over my face? I truly believe she was capable of anything.

I don't know how long I sat next to her body pondering events but when I eventually got up from her side and went back upstairs my knees were stiff from sitting for so long. I climbed the ladder into her loft and carefully crawled across the narrow boards. I picked up the piece of board that she'd used to cover the hole on her side of the wall and took it into my loft and hid it underneath some boxes and old sheets. I then went back into her loft and began putting the pile of bricks that Diana had taken out of the wall through the hole into my loft. I then crawled back through and carefully rebuilt the wall with the bricks. It took me quite a while and wasn't helped by having to do it using just my phone light. I had to juggle the bricks around to make them fit properly so had to rebuild parts of it several times. I had to keep reminding myself that there was no need to rush but my heart was racing because I just wanted to get it done. By the time I'd finished, the wall wasn't perfect but to the casual observer and from a distance, it would be near impossible to tell that there'd once been a gap there. I'm hoping that the police won't feel the need to look further and will assume that Diana suffered a tragic accident whilst she was putting something in her loft. When her body is eventually discovered it will no doubt be assumed that it was a terrible accident – which it was – and there'll be nothing to suggest that anyone else was present.

So why didn't I call the emergency services?

Because I can't face it.

There would be endless questions and the very fact that I was there would raise suspicions. Even though there is some evidence of sorts – the hole in the wall, the anti-depressants – in themselves, they prove nothing because who's to say that I didn't do it all myself? I can't prove that she put the vile comments about Tom and his family on my Facebook account or that she came into my house and drugged me. I can only assume that she looked at my previous Facebook history and somehow guessed at our connection but would the police believe that? It sounds like a far-fetched conspiracy theory and totally ridiculous, but more importantly, they're going to want to know why she did it. I can't explain to myself why Diana tried to destroy me so how can I expect someone else to believe me? The explanation that a seemingly normal woman is quite mad and has a vendetta against me is not going to cut it.

Had she been alive and injured, I would have helped her, but really, what's to be gained by involving myself? All it would achieve would be to blacken a dead women's name or, if I can't convince the police to believe my version of events it could involve me in something that could end in dire consequences for me. I don't have any faith that the police will believe that Diana has done these things because my own brother thought I was mentally ill and imagining things. The very fact that I was in Diana's house and she's dead would not look good.

No, as far as anyone else is concerned, I know nothing.

* * *

In an attempt to stop myself from pacing around and dwelling on recent events – which is what I did yesterday – after I've eaten my lunch I decide that the house needs a good clean. Diana only died the day before yesterday and realistically, it could be some time until her body is discovered. I need to continue with my life as if nothing has happened.

I dust and polish the entire house as if my life depends on it and the house is spotless and gleaming. I then set about the floors with the vacuum cleaner and have just finished my bedroom and am coiling the lead around the handle when movement catches my eye through the bedroom window. A middle-aged woman is walking up Diana's garden path to her front door.

I stand to the side of the window, out of sight, to watch her. I haven't seen the woman before and

I wonder who she is. I get as close to the window as possible and can just see the top of the her head as she rings the bell and waits. The top light of my window is ajar and after a moment I hear her banging the letter box impatiently. After several moments she stoops down and I realise what she's doing.

She's looking through the letter box.

I watch as she suddenly jumps backwards from the front door. Her hand is clamped over her mouth and her eyes are wide in shock. After several minutes she opens her handbag and fumbles around before pulling out a mobile phone. I silently step backwards from the window being careful not to make any noise or attract her attention. She's obviously seen Diana's body in the hallway and is ringing the emergency services. Of course I knew that Diana would be found, but I didn't think it would be so quickly.

I take a deep breath and try to stay calm.

There's nothing to be afraid of, I tell myself, I've done nothing wrong.

So why do I feel so guilty?

CHAPTER TWENTY-SIX

Five months later

The van's parked in the road outside next door and I watch through the lounge window as the middle-aged man closes up the back doors of the van, walks around to the front of the vehicle, climbs into the cab and zooms off. It's a rental van going by the writing on the side of the van so no doubt has to be returned on time otherwise they'll be charged for another day.

The light is starting to fade already even though it's not yet six o'clock. This time next week it'll be dark when the clocks have gone back an hour. I've caught sight of my new neighbours as they've scurried in and out of the house carrying boxes; a young couple with long, lean limbs and big smiles. I'm guessing that the van driver was a relative;

maybe one of their dad's. Over the months since Diana's death I've often wondered if her house would be sold to a first-time buyer and, judging by the smallish amount of furniture that's come out of the removal van, I think it has.

Do they know the history of the house they've just bought? Knowing how garrulous estate agents are, I suspect that they do. Although it would be easy enough to find the details online as Diana's death made the headlines of the local newspaper and was repeated many times on the local radio news.

As it transpired, I needn't have worried at all about the police questioning me over Diana's death. The interview consisted of a harassed looking young policeman sitting in my lounge for all of ten minutes and barely looking at me as he scribbled my replies to his *routine enquiries*. When had I seen her last and had I heard anything, seemed to be the gist of it. He gave me the impression that accidentally falling through the floor of the loft was to be expected if you were foolish enough to go up there once you'd reached the grand old age of fifty-two. I laughed when he referred to Diana as *elderly* and had to cover my snort of laughter with a cough. There's a saying that policeman look younger every day and to my eyes he looked as if he was barely old enough to shave.

I did manage to find out that the woman I'd seen at Diana's door was a work colleague. She'd come round as Diana had missed an important meeting and, unable to contact her by phone and knowing that she lived alone, a welfare visit was hastily arranged to ensure that she was okay. Diana worked at a local engineering company as an administrator and I must admit that I'm impressed at what a caring company they seem to be.

She must have been a better employee than a neighbour.

Once Diana's body had been removed, her house was closed up and it remained that way for several months. Somehow, Bert always seems to be in the know with the current gossip and he kept me informed as to what was going on. Apparently Diana didn't have any close family at all and as she hadn't made a will the house ended up in the hands of a distant cousin.

I'd have felt sorry for her if she wasn't so horrible.

A woof from behind me makes me jump and I turn around and look down into Barkely's little face looking up at me. I don't know how, but somehow he can tell the time and he wants his dinner. I lean down and ruffle his ears.

'All right, fella, it's coming up.'

I go out to the kitchen and Barkely trots behind me and sits patiently whilst I take his bowl out of the cupboard and fill it with his biscuit and half a tin of dog food. He's been staying here for the last two weeks and he's no trouble at all, in fact I'm considering getting a dog of my own as I rather like having a little companion. Bert is in Australia for another five weeks so I have my furry house guest for quite a while longer and I just know that I'm going to miss him when he returns to his home next door.

I place Barkely's bowl on the floor and watch as he almost inhales it. In mere minutes the bowl is licked clean and Barkley looks up at me expectantly.

'That's it, boy,' I say, holding my hands up and laughing. 'Your dad won't thank me if he comes back and you're twice the size you were before he went away.'

Once I'd offered to dog sit Barkley, Bert couldn't wait to book his airplane ticket to visit his daughter. We've never discussed Diana but I've noticed a marked change in him since she died; he's always out in his garden and seems much more relaxed now that she's not here. I'm sure she was bullying him, too. When I think back, he was always on edge when she was around, and definitely less friendly to me. I remember the black bruise that was on his arm and I can't help but think that she did it; that it was punishment for him being friendly to me. I don't know how one middle-aged woman can make such a difference but I do know that in the months since she's died, I've seen and spoken to more of my neighbours in this street than I ever did whilst she was alive. Did she really blight the lives of the whole street? I'll never know but even though it sounds awful, I'm glad she's no longer here.

And I'm not the only one.

I called into the jewellery shop where Jayne works a few weeks after Diana died. I was sure that she would have seen the news of her death in the newspaper but I wanted to be sure that she knew; she *needed* to know so that she could move on with her life.

Jayne was standing behind the counter when I entered the shop and as soon as I saw her, I could see that she was already aware of Diana's death. She was standing tall – not the hunched, *make me invisible* stance that she had before and when she realised who I was she smiled broadly and seemed happy to see me. How are you, she asked, as if we were old friends, and I told her I was fine and asked how she was. Good, she said, she was in the process of house hunting but stressed that this time she was looking for a detached, she even hinted that she was *seeing someone* but that it was *early days*. There was no sign of the nervous hysteria that was apparent on our last meeting. I told her about Diana and she said she'd seen it in the local newspaper. Neither of us pretended that it was tragic or sad and a knowing look passed between us. Part of me wanted to tell her about the loft, and how Diana had been able to get into the house but of course, I couldn't, and really what would have been gained?

I go to the fridge and pull out the remains of the lasagne I made yesterday and pop it into the oven to reheat. Ben came for a visit and I'd made such a lot of food that even he couldn't eat it all. He's picking up the keys to his house next week; he sold his flat in super quick time and he'll be moving back here to live – just ten minutes drive from me. I teased him that he'll be buying a pipe and slippers soon to go with his three bed detached and he laughed and said that he might get the slippers but not the pipe, as he doesn't want to start smoking again.

I've nearly told him about the loft so many times but always manage to stop myself. There's no doubt that I would feel a sense of relief at being able to tell the truth at last but I know that the relief would be fleeting and I would soon regret sharing my secret. It's in the past and that's where it's going to stay and I know that with time, the urge to confess will pass. As far as Ben is aware I'm much better now – a result of the weekly counselling I've told him that I'm attending.

I set the oven timer for thirty-five minutes then fill the kettle with water and put it on to boil. I take two mugs down from the cupboard and arrange them on a tray with a small carton of milk. I place an unopened packet of chocolate biscuits on the tray and then spoon instant coffee into the mugs. Once the kettle boils I pour boiling water over the coffee and carefully carry the tray out into the hall.

'I won't be long, Barkely,' I say, as I open the front door whilst balancing the tray in one hand. Barkley cocks his head to one side and watches me from the kitchen.

'I'm just popping next door,' I say to him as if he can understand me. I pull the front door closed behind me and walk down the path and along the pavement in front of the houses before turning into my new next door neighbour's garden. The gate has been left ajar and I walk up the path to their front door.

I take a deep breath and knock on their front door.

It's time to meet my new neighbours.

THE END

Thank you so much for reading this book, I really do appreciate it. I do hope that you've enjoyed it and if you have, please leave a review or star rating on Amazon/and or Goodreads.